"I want more children.

"I want a wife I can love with my whole soul. But if I never find a woman I can feel that way about, then I'll stay a bachelor. No matter what, I'm going to be the best father in the world to my three girls," Spencer said.

There was no doubt in Alexandra's mind that he would do just that. Emotion gathered in her throat and was nearly choking her, but she had no time for regret or sentiment. She would help him with the girls while she still could, while he still liked and trusted her, and then she'd get out of his life before she made an even bigger mess of it.

"Forget I asked you to talk to the girls for me. I completely understand you not wanting to get involved in our family matters," Spencer said.

I'm already more involved than you know....

Dear Reader,

Welcome to another month of life and love in the backyards, big cities and wide open spaces of Harlequin American Romance! When April showers keep you indoors, you'll stay snug and dry with our four wonderful new stories.

You've heard of looking for love in the wrong places—but what happens when the "wrong" place turns out to be the right one? In Charlotte Maclay's newest miniseries, two sisters are about to find out...when each one wakes up to find herself CAUGHT WITH A COWBOY! We start off this month with Ella's story, *The Right Cowboy's Bed*.

And hold on to your hats, because you're invited to a whirlwind *Last-Minute Marriage*. With her signature sparkling humor, Karen Toller Whittenburg tells the delightful story of a man who must instantly produce the perfect family he's been writing about.

Everyone loves the sight of a big strong man wrapped around a little child's finger, and we can't wait to introduce you to our two new fathers. Dr. Spencer Jones's life changes forever when he inherits three little girls and opens his heart to love in Emily Dalton's *A Precious Inheritance*. And no one blossoms more beautifully than a woman who's WITH CHILD... as Graham Richards soon discovers after one magical night in *Having the Billionaire's Baby* by Anne Haven, the second story in this extra-special promotion.

At American Romance, we're dedicated to bringing you stories that will warm your heart and brighten your day. Enjoy!

Warm wishes,
Melissa Jeglinski
Associate Senior Editor

A Precious Inheritance

EMILY DALTON

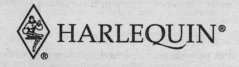

HARLEQUIN®

TORONTO • NEW YORK • LONDON
AMSTERDAM • PARIS • SYDNEY • HAMBURG
STOCKHOLM • ATHENS • TOKYO • MILAN • MADRID
PRAGUE • WARSAW • BUDAPEST • AUCKLAND

To Jane Jordan Browne, agent extraordinaire.
Thanks for your years of support and guidance
and those great grapefruits every Christmas!
Here's hoping we've got many more years of success
ahead in the New Millennium.

ISBN 0-373-16823-3

A PRECIOUS INHERITANCE

Copyright © 2000 by Danice Jo Allen.

ABOUT THE AUTHOR

Emily Dalton lives in the beautiful foothills of Bountiful, Utah, with her husband of twenty-one years, two teenage sons and a very spoiled American Eskimo dog named Juno. She has written several Regency and historical novels, and now thoroughly enjoys writing contemporary romances for Harlequin American Romance. She loves old movies, Jane Austen and traveling by train. Her biggest weaknesses are chocolate truffles and crafts boutiques.

Books by Emily Dalton

HARLEQUIN AMERICAN ROMANCE

Don't miss any of our special offers. Write to us at the following address for information on our newest releases.

Harlequin Reader Service
U.S.: 3010 Walden Ave., P.O. Box 1325, Buffalo, NY 14269
Canadian: P.O. Box 609, Fort Erie, Ont. L2A 5X3

The Misses
Elizabeth, Margaret and Camilla Rose
invite you to join them at the
Jonesville Community Church on
Monday, January 1,
at ten o'clock in the morning,
to celebrate the wedding of their daddy,
Dr. Spencer Jones
to
Ms. Alexandra Ethington.

This is the first official step toward
our becoming a real family!
On January 2 we're going to the county
courthouse to finalize our adoption to
Dr. and Mrs. Jones…who, to us,
are already Mommy and Daddy.

Please come to Gran's house after the
ceremony to see what heaven looks like.
P.S. Don't worry, there'll be cake, too!

Chapter One

"I can't be pregnant, Dr. Jones. It's...it's *impossible!*"

Spencer leaned forward, threaded his long fingers together and rested his hands on the desk. He gazed into the eyes of the shell-shocked woman seated in the chair opposite him and suggested, "Impossible is a pretty strong word, Kathy. And completely inaccurate in this case. You're at least three months along."

"But...I'm forty-two years old! And Pete's *forty-six!*"

Spencer smiled. "Not exactly ready for the Shady Acres Rest Home. And still spry enough, evidently, to have sex on a frequent basis."

Kathy blushed and hid an involuntary grin, which was answer enough for Spencer. He'd been taking care of the Andersons and their kids since he took over his grandfather's practice five years ago and, by all appearances, he figured Kathy and Pete to be as much in love now as the day they'd married. He had no doubt that the physical side of their relationship was as regular as the mailman. They had five kids—and one more on the way—to prove it.

"Don't be embarrassed, Kathy. I think it's great that you and Pete have such a healthy relationship. I'm just surprised that, since you seemed satisfied with the size of your family, you weren't using protection. Didn't I give you a prescription for a low-dose birth control pill?"

"Yes, but I never had it filled. I thought I was too old to get pregnant," she confessed, teary-eyed. "I've been irregular for a couple of years now."

"That doesn't mean you can't get pregnant."

She sighed. "Guess not."

"You're very healthy. I don't anticipate a problem with the pregnancy at all."

She bit her lip and nodded.

Spencer waited, then asked gently, "Don't you want the baby, Kathy?"

Her head reared up, her eyes wide. "Oh, I *do* want the baby, Dr. Jones. You know how crazy I am about the rest of my tribe. I'm just…well… feeling kind of bowled over right now. My youngest starts high school this year. What will my kids say?" She laughed shakily. "What will Pete say? I feel so *stupid!*"

Spencer stood up, straightened his bright-green Tasmanian Devil tie with a smooth motion, then walked around the desk to lay a hand on Kathy's shoulder. "Once your kids get used to the idea of a little brother or sister, they'll be fighting over who gets to hold him. You have built-in baby-sitters. And I'll bet a truckload of tongue depressors that Pete's going to be thrilled when he hears the news."

Kathy gripped Spencer's hand and gave him a watery smile. "What in the world would I want with a truckload of tongue depressors? Let's wager something useful, like the same amount of disposable diapers. You're probably right, but if things don't work out the way you think they will, can I send Pete and the kids in to see you? You talk sense better than anyone I know, Dr. Jones. And people listen, despite those silly ties you wear!''

"Say, if I remember right, you added to my collection of silly ties last Christmas with one that was covered with pint-size penguin angels.''

"I plead guilty. But it was Pete who picked it out.''

Spencer chuckled and gave Kathy's hand a quick squeeze, then picked up her chart from the desk. "And you think you two are too old for more kids! But send 'em in—the whole tribe if you want—and I'll talk to them. I don't think it will be necessary, though, because once the surprise wears off they'll probably all accept the fact that you're pregnant and be more supportive than you ever dreamed possible. In fact, this might be the easiest pregnancy you've ever had. They'll probably wait on you hand and foot.''

Kathy burst out laughing. "That'll be the day!''

Spencer watched Kathy leave the office moments later with a nervous but happy smile on her lips, her purse stuffed with vitamin samples and appointment cards for an ultrasound at the hospital and a return visit. Since he'd gently prodded her into an improved state of mind, she would do a much better job breaking the news to her family and putting a positive spin on it. Sure, the pregnancy was a surprise, but he believed what he'd told Kathy was true. The whole family would be crazy about the kid in no time at all. Now if *he'd* received a similar surprise...

Spencer smiled wryly and shook his head. He hated surprises. And, as a bachelor, sudden unexpected parenthood would be right up there with the worst kind of surprises he could think of.

As he finished filling out Kathy's chart and picked up the folder containing the medical records of his next patient, Velma entered the room and headed for the small refrigerator by the window for her daily afternoon hit of diet soda.

Short and stocky, she wore her usual uniform of black hose and patent-leather shoes with a white skirt and knee-length lab jacket. Her teased-up hairdo was dyed as black as her hose, and a pair of enormous pale-pink tortoiseshell glasses that perched on the end of her small nose magnified her eyes, which were made up sixties-style. In fact, with the black eyeliner extended like fishtails, her eyes behind the oversize glasses resembled tropical fish in fishbowls.

But despite her retro look, Velma was an excellent office manager and physician's assistant, as well as a good person and friend. She'd worked for his grandfather for ten years before Spencer took over and she'd been invaluable to him during those first few weeks of practice. She knew everyone in the small town of Jonesville, New Hampshire, and had made the transition from old, trusted Dr. Jones to young, untried Dr. Jones go as slick as an oil spill. Not, however, that the transition would have been that difficult for the townspeople in the first place. After all, Spencer came from accepted stock.

When Spencer's beloved grandfather, Benjamin

Jones, died at the age of seventy-eight, still active and practicing medicine when a sudden stroke took him away painlessly and fast, the town had been thrown into a tizzy of despair and anxiety. Who could possibly take the place of their own dear Dr. Jones?

Everyone knew Ben's son, David, had become a dermatologist. A fancy-schmancy sort, he'd moved to Boston, then retired early to Florida to play golf and go on Caribbean cruises, threatening the tradition of always having a Dr. Jones in town since the founding father, Josiah Jones, first wielded a knife to carve out the appendix of a local trapper.

The story went that the knife had been used for cleaning fish and skinning rabbits just moments before, but Josiah washed it in scalding water, dipped it in a jar of moonshine whiskey, poured half of what was left down the throat of his patient, then gulped down the remaining liquor himself.

With a natural talent for doctoring and a medical journal to guide him, the operation was a success. But it occurred to him that it might be a whole lot easier helping sick folks if he had the proper equipment at hand. He immediately ordered everything he needed from Boston and, a few weeks later, drove a wagon into Lancaster, the nearest town of any size, to pick up his supplies.

Since that momentous day, the Jones family turned out a doctor or two every generation. One of them always settled in Jonesville as a general practitioner, delivering babies, removing warts, prying popcorn kernels out of toddlers' noses and dispensing advice about everything from nail biting to impotence.

Spencer never intended to follow in his grandfather's footsteps. He'd agreed to fill in till the practice could be sold to someone more suited to small-town life. After all, he'd been raised in Boston and had been practicing there as an internal medicine specialist for nearly a year. But after a few weeks, Spencer had known he belonged in Jonesville, not in Boston, and he'd moved into the house right next door to his grandmother's, just four blocks from the office on the corner of Maple and Main.

Besides being grandson of the old Doc Jones, Spencer had the advantage in winning over the town's confidence and approval by being his grandfather's spitting image. He was just as tall and lean as his grandfather, had the same lanky gait as he walked down the street from house to office and had the same straight blond hair and blue eyes that Benjamin Jones had had as a younger man. Some said Spencer even sounded like his granddad.

The one big difference in them was the way they dressed. Spencer wore the obligatory white lab coat, of course, but his trousers were usually khakis or corduroys, his shoes comfortable loafers, and his shirts various colors of the rainbow. As for his ties… Well, he was famous for those. He claimed that wearing bright, sometimes downright gaudy ties gave the patients something to look at, laugh at and talk about while he did the necessary poking around to arrive at a diagnosis. Over the years he'd acquired quite a collection of novelty ties—such as the Tasmanian Devil tie he was presently wearing—as gifts from his patients.

"Dr. Jones? There's a call for you."

Immersed in the history of his next patient, Spencer hadn't even heard the phone ring. He looked up just long enough to make brief eye contact, his head still full of medical jargon and lab tests. "Unless it's an emergency, Velma, please take a message. Mr. Hansen's already been waiting several minutes."

"It's a Mr. Liebermann, calling from Boston. He says he's a lawyer and has urgent business with you that deals with someone named…Karlie Ethington? He's very insistent, Dr. Jones, and—"

But Spencer needed no further persuasion to take the call. He dropped Mr. Hansen's file on the desk and took the receiver out of Velma's hand.

"Yes? This is Dr. Jones."

"Dr. Spencer Jones?"

"Yes. Why are you calling me about Karlie?"

There was a pause on the other end of the line, then, "Dr. Jones, I have some bad news."

Spencer felt his stomach tightening into one big knot. It would be silly to call the feeling he had a premonition because what was coming was just too obvious. "Karlie's dead, isn't she?"

"Yes, I'm afraid so, Dr. Jones. She and her husband were killed in a plane crash in Switzerland last week."

Spencer was silent. Maybe he would have known what to say if he'd been able to define how he was feeling. But how did one feel about a former high school sweetheart, a woman who on the eve of their wedding six years ago wrote him a note informing him that she'd met someone new and was on a plane to Las Vegas that very night to exchange vows in some drive-through Chapel of Luv? Someone new who also just happened to be stinking rich with Massachusetts old money and imbued with the prestige of forbears who caught their first glimpse of America from the decks of the *Mayflower?*

Karlie had stuck with him through high school, med school, his internship and residency, but when Spencer was ready to hang his shingle, she'd dumped him. Needless to say, her sudden desertion had been a shock, and extremely painful.

Spencer had forgiven Karlie long ago, but the little trick she'd played on him that night before their wedding had left him with a permanent distaste for surprises and taught him to be gun-shy when it came to slipping diamond rings on female fingers.

"Dr. Jones?"

"I'm sorry. I'm just shocked. And very sorry." His brows furrowed as it occurred to him that there was something odd about this whole proceeding. "But why are you calling *me?*" As a matter of fact, why would anyone call him about Karlie's death? He'd been out of her life for six years, had never once had any sort of contact with her.

"You're named in Mrs. Ethington's will. I'm calling to inform you where and when to meet for the reading and offer you transportation at our expense."

Spencer shook his head, disbelieving. "This is crazy. Why would *I* be in Karlie's will?"

"In fact, Dr. Jones..." Mr. Liebermann cleared his throat before continuing. "Mrs. Ethington and her husband, Richard Ethington the Third, have...er...left you...er...something."

"What is it?" he asked bluntly. "Just tell me over the phone. I have no intention of accepting money, or anything else, for that matter. Maybe Karlie thought she owed me something. I don't know, but—''

''I'll have a private jet waiting for you at the Lancaster airport. It's very important that you meet with us at our offices this Friday afternoon, July 24, at three o'clock.''

''Who else will be there?'' Spencer just wanted an idea of exactly how uncomfortable this meeting was going to be.

''Just Mr. Ethington's father, Richard Ethington the Second.''

''What about *Mrs.* Ethington the Second?''

''There is no current Mrs. Ethington. Mr. Ethington is divorced, and his first wife, who was the mother of the deceased Richard Ethington the Third, is also deceased.''

''What about Karlie's parents?''

''They declined to be in attendance.''

''They *declined?* Why?'' Although he didn't have the slightest desire to see Karlie's weird parents again, he thought it was very strange that they wouldn't be at the reading of their only daughter's last will and testament.

''They...er...had their reasons, Dr. Jones, and I'll explain them on Friday, if you don't mind.''

''And if I do mind?''

''I'm sorry, Dr. Jones. I've said all I'm going to say at this juncture.''

Again Spencer was silent. Mingled with the real sadness he felt over Karlie's sudden and early death was an irritation that he was going to be somehow dragged into something he had no business being part of. But the fact that Karlie had thought to include him in her will found a soft spot in his heart he'd probably always have for her. He supposed going to Boston to hear what she'd left him was the least he could do.

Probably it was old love letters, or poems he'd written during math class when all he could concentrate on was Karlie, three seats up, and the curve of her cheek when she turned her face toward the window. Or maybe it was the class ring he'd given her when they'd first agreed to go steady. Or maybe it was that purple stuffed pig he'd won for her at the county fair. As long as it wasn't money or something valuable, he'd take it. He supposed he wouldn't mind accepting a last memento of affection from Karlie.

But what about the husband, Richard Ethington the Third? What could *he* have left for his wife's old boyfriend? A poisonous pet snake?

"Dr. Jones, are you still there?"

"Yes. But before I agree to come to this meeting Friday afternoon, I have one more question. What did Karlie's husband leave—"

"All your questions will be answered on Friday, Doctor…"

"But—"

"Please. You're just wasting your time and mine. Will we see you there?"

Spencer sighed deeply. "Yes, I'll be there."

"Excellent. Now, as for transportation to our law offices…"

Spencer wrote down all the information about the private jet that would transport him from the small Lancaster airport to Logan Airport in Boston, and the limo that would be waiting for him there. When the surreal conversation with Mr. Liebermann was concluded, he hung up the phone and turned to Velma, who was standing at his elbow, a look of intense curiosity on her face. "We're going to have to reschedule my Friday afternoon appointments."

"That much I gathered," she said with a brisk nod. "Are you going to tell me the rest? Seems to me you could use a good listener about now."

Spencer picked up Mr. Hansen's medical file, tapped it against the edge of the desk, then gave Velma a grateful smile. "Sure. We'll talk. I'd like that. But not till all the patients are gone. In the meantime, please start working on Friday's schedule."

IN THE LIMO ON THE WAY to the law offices of Liebermann, Copinger and Swartz, Spencer's mind was going round and round like a squirrel in a cage. The private jet and the limo with its posh leather interior and uniformed chauffeur had just added to his disquiet. If Richard Ethington the Third's lawyers were rich enough to transport unimportant, nonpaying clients like himself in such luxury, he could just imagine the size of the family fortune.

Hell, if Karlie had left him money it would ruin everything...all the good memories and then some. He didn't want money. And if she'd thought money could somehow make up for what she'd done to him, he'd be forced to believe money had been her motive for leaving him in the first place. He'd much rather believe she'd left him for love. Sappy, sure, but more palatable than believing your high school sweetheart had been a gold digger.

As the limo pulled next to the curb, Spencer rebuttoned his double-breasted gray suit—accessorized with a subdued, solid-color maroon tie for a change—and stepped out of the limo before the chauffeur could open the door for him. He felt silly being treated like a dignitary or a rock star.

The towering building, with its tinted glass façade, was imposing. He had to check in at the desk in the main lobby. The elevator had an attendant. Security cameras hung conspicuously from the ceilings. It seemed every move one made in the building was monitored and escorted. He was beginning to wonder if he'd be allowed to visit the washroom without a hall pass!

The thickly carpeted hallway on the 28th floor muffled his footsteps as a female secretary led him to a mahogany-paneled double door just as the clock struck three. She preceded him inside and announced him as if he were arriving at a royal ball, then discreetly slipped into the background, as quiet and unobtrusive as a servant in one of those Jane Austen period movies.

Spencer observed four "suits" sitting around a board table. They all turned to look at him, none of them appearing happy to see him and one of them looking mad as hell. Ah, thought Spencer, that would be Richard Ethington the Second, Karlie's father-in-law. Stands to reason he wouldn't be especially thrilled to see one of Karlie's ex-boyfriends at the reading of his son and daughter-in-law's wills. And Spencer couldn't blame him.

"Dr. Jones." A thin, balding man with a neatly trimmed mustache stood up and moved to Spencer with his hand outstretched, but with no welcoming smile. After a brief, firm handshake, he turned and introduced Spencer to the rest of the room's occupants.

Two of the men were Copinger and Swartz, the other partners in the firm, both as poker-faced as Liebermann. The remaining occupant, the gray-haired, stout-chested man who seemed to pulsate hostility and suspicion, was, indeed, Richard Ethington the Second. The lawyers stood to shake Spencer's hand, but Ethington stayed glued to his chair. Liebermann indicated a seat directly across from Ethington, and Spencer sat down.

Once reseated himself, Liebermann wasted no time. ''I'll begin with what I consider—indeed, what both Mr. and Mrs. Ethington considered—the most important business of this day, the guardianship of their three daughters, Elizabeth Ann, Margaret Emily, and Camilla Rose Ethington, ages, respectively, five years, four years, and nine months.'' He shuffled his papers and cleared his throat, then pulled off his glasses, extracted a white handkerchief from his jacket pocket and began to clean the lenses with slow, precise deliberation.

For someone so eager to begin, it seemed odd that Mr. Liebermann now appeared to be stalling. Spencer's mind raced as he waited. Since hearing of Karlie's death, he'd wondered if she'd had children and how the tragedy of their parents' death would affect them. Now he wondered if Karlie had been a hands-on kind of parent, or if the pressures of being a socialite had made her rely on a nanny for most of the children's care.

He glanced at the Ethington orphans' grim-faced granddad and wondered where Karlie's parents were and who of the two sets of grandparents would be granted guardianship of the girls. He'd always thought Karlie's parents were off the wall—always trying new and wild ways to "find" themselves— so they might not be the best choice…unless, of course, they'd changed and become more settled over the past six years. He just hoped the kids got a fair shake at having a halfway normal life.

As Spencer watched Liebermann continue to fuss with his glasses, he questioned why these big city lawyers couldn't have arranged the meeting so that inconsequential bequests like his were taken care of first, then the more important and personal stuff could be discussed after his departure. But, apparently, no one but him had thought of such a sensible sequence of events.

Resigned, Spencer took a sip from a glass of water the shadowlike secretary had unobtrusively slid in front of him, but choked on the first swallow. "This is gin!" he exclaimed. "Isn't it kind of early in the day for hard liquor?"

"The gin was my idea," Mr. Swartz confessed quietly. "I ordered it for you and Mr. Ethington because I thought you both might need a drink before this meeting is over."

Ethington slammed his fist on the table and spoke for the first time. "Damn it! I *knew* it! That idiot son of mine has given away half the Ethington fortune, hasn't he? I knew I should never have given him complete control over his inheritance before I'd officially kicked the bucket, but he—"

"Mr. Ethington," Liebermann interrupted, "you're jumping to conclusions. *Erroneous* conclusions, I might add. Please be patient and let me continue."

Ethington growled something under his breath, crossed his arms and fell silent.

Now Spencer was getting nervous. *Really* nervous. If Ethington's conclusions were erroneous, and a nobody from rural New Hampshire like himself becoming an instant and unwilling millionaire wasn't the reason they both needed gin at three o'clock in the afternoon, what *was* the reason?

"I'll continue now," Mr. Liebermann said wearily, then resolutely adjusted his glasses one last time and picked up the documents. He gave Spencer and Mr. Ethington a severe look. "And please, gentlemen, no further outbursts."

Liebermann's warning against outbursts did nothing to lessen Spencer's anxiety. Every muscle in his body seemed to bunch with dread.

Liebermann took a long breath, then began, "As clearly delineated in both of their wills, in the event of Mr. and Mrs. Ethington passing away together— such as did, indeed, occur—Mr. Richard Ethington the Third and Mrs. Karlie Ethington expressly wished for, and have made legal provisions to accomplish, the granting of full guardianship of their three children to…Dr. Spencer Jones."

"What?" bellowed Mr. Ethington as he shot to his feet. "That's impossible!"

"I'm afraid not, Mr. Ethington. It's right here in black and white and repeated, word for word, in Mrs. Karlie Ethington's will." Liebermann laid the document flat on the desk and pointed to the paragraph he'd just read. "You may read it yourself, if you wish."

Ethington grabbed the document, his face growing redder and redder as he fumbled for his reading glasses.

Mr. Liebermann turned to Spencer. "You may read it, too, if you wish, Dr. Jones."

Spencer swallowed against a throat that had gone tinder dry. He was beyond amazement. He was stunned speechless. He could only stare at Mr. Liebermann and wonder if he was dreaming.

"When were these wills drawn up?" Ethington demanded to know, his angry and disbelieving gaze still fixed on the sentences that apparently bequeathed his grandchildren to a stranger. Spencer couldn't blame him for such a reaction. He'd be angry, too.

"Just after their youngest child, Camilla Rose, was born. They updated their wills after the birth of each child."

"Well, haven't you got anything to say, Jones?" Ethington threw the document to the desk directly in front of Spencer. "You must have known about this. You must have agreed to this arrangement. But why? For the Ethington money, I suppose? For the trust funds?"

Indignant, Spencer finally found his voice. "I knew nothing about this. I didn't agree to be guardian of Karlie's children, and I don't give a damn about the Ethington money!"

Ethington propped his hands on the desk and leaned toward Spencer. "They're not just Karlie's children! They're my son's children, too. They're *my* grandchildren! You're nothing at all to those three little girls."

Spencer took a long swallow from his glass of gin, then stood up and assumed the same glowering pose as Mr. Ethington. "Don't you think I know that? I haven't got a clue why your son and my ex-girlfriend named me guardian. It's impractical. No, it's more than that, it's preposterous! Hell, I'm a bachelor! Besides, the girls should be with someone they know. Someone they're used to already. Someone they love."

"That would be difficult to accomplish, Dr. Jones," Mr. Liebermann observed quietly.

Spencer waved a hand in Ethington's direction. "What about their grandfather? What about Karlie's parents?"

Mr. Liebermann flitted a nervous glance at Mr. Ethington. "Mr. Ethington and his son have not been on speaking terms for three years. The little girls know him no better than they know you."

"But I'm still their grandfather," Ethington blustered. "I'm still their flesh and blood and that must count for something!"

Mr. Liebermann's left eye twitched, but he ignored Mr. Ethington and continued. "As for Mrs. Ethington's parents, they moved to Pago Pago and haven't seen their daughter since just a few months after the wedding. It's my understanding that they've become…er…nudists and naturalists. When I was finally able to contact them through friends of theirs who own a telephone, they expressed deep regret on their daughter's passing but had no wish to be in attendance at the reading of the will. All financial bequests to them from their daughter I have been instructed to give to various animal preservation charities."

Spencer sat down again, slowly and carefully, his

mind reeling. "But surely there's still someone who would be better at raising those kids than me."

"You're damned right about that," Mr. Ethington snarled, then lifted his glass of gin and drained it.

Spencer shook his head. "They wouldn't have a mother, and I work long, sometimes unpredictable hours."

"I understand you have relatives in Jonesville, Dr. Jones. Perhaps they could help with child care responsibilities," Mr. Liebermann suggested.

"My relatives in Jonesville are either too busy or too elderly to take on the care of three small children."

"Er…what about your grandmother? I had heard—that is, I thought I understood that she was in excellent health."

"She's nearly seventy-five. And besides that, she has a life of her own!"

Mr. Liebermann tapped his pen against the desk and pursed his lips. "Yes, well, surely a doctor could afford to pay for child care."

"Surely, there's a better solution for this problem than that," Spencer returned irritably. "Those girls deserve the best home situation possible. If Karlie and her husband didn't feel comfortable giving guardianship of their children to someone in their own family, there are thousands of wonderful people out there dying to adopt."

Ethington's fist hit the table again. "I won't allow anyone to raise those girls but me! No one's going to adopt them, especially you, Jones!"

"Don't you get it, Ethington? I don't want to adopt them. I just want what's best for them." He turned to Mr. Liebermann. "Since I didn't agree to this in the first place, I can refuse to take the girls, can't I?"

"Of course you can refuse," Mr. Liebermann agreed with a careful nod of his head. "But before you make your final decision, Dr. Jones, there's a letter here from Mrs. Ethington which, perhaps, contains an explanation for this extraordinary entrustment." He pulled a legal-size envelope out from under a stack of papers and handed it to Spencer, then stood up. "I suggest we all retire to the adjacent boardroom so that Dr. Jones can read the letter in private."

"This is crazy!" Mr. Ethington declared. "I'm not going anywhere until this is settled!"

Spencer eyed the envelope warily. It was Karlie's handwriting on the front, all right. "Liebermann, do you know what the letter says?"

"No, but if it has the power to help determine your decision, you'll probably need some quiet time to think." He looked pointedly, if briefly, at Mr. Ethington. "That will be impossible unless all occupants, except yourself, leave the room. We'll return in ten minutes for your final decision. And it *will* be your final decision, Dr. Jones. There'll be no turning back."

Ethington's face went nearly purple with fury and frustration. "But I demand—"

Mr. Liebermann directed the secretary to take Ethington's arm and gently urge him toward the exit. "I'm sorry, sir, but you're in no position to demand anything at the moment. You can contest the will if you wish, but today's proceedings are legally binding until such time as a court of law decides otherwise."

"I won't stand for this—!"

As soon as the door clicked shut behind the others, reducing Ethington's rants to a muffle, Spencer sat down, slid his thumb under the glued edge of the envelope and opened it. Inside was a single sheet of stationery—yellow, Karlie's favorite color. A bittersweet ache flowered in his chest. He unfolded the letter and began to read Karlie's familiar handwriting. "Dear Spence…"

Two minutes later, Spencer refolded the letter, slipped it into an inside pocket of his suit jacket, sank into a chair and stared at the wall across from the table. Eight minutes later, Mr. Liebermann stuck his head in the door and asked, "Dr. Jones, have you made a decision, or do you need more time?"

Spencer dragged his gaze away from the wall and looked Mr. Liebermann squarely in the eye. His answer was quiet and firm. "What do I have to do to make those children legally mine?"

Chapter Two

Alexandra K. Ethington was up to her chin in hot water and fragrant bubbles when the doorbell rang. She opened her eyes and glanced at the travel clock on the vanity, resting amid the cluttered contents of her overnight bag.

"Criminy," she muttered under her breath. "Has it already been an hour since he called?" But perhaps someone else was at the door, she rationalized. Someone she could ignore.

Alex's eyes were drifting shut again, when a loud, insistent banging on the front door convinced her that whoever was on the other side wasn't about to be ignored. And Richard Ethington the Second fit that description perfectly.

"Coming, Dad," she called, as she pulled herself out of the soothing, scented water and stepped onto the plush rug into which her damp toes sunk a good two inches. It had been so long since she'd enjoyed such luxuries, she felt downright hedonistic. But after six months of roach-infested hotels and cold showers—when she could get them at all—interspersed with mud-coated tents and moldy sleeping bags in the deepest parts of rural China, she felt perfectly justified in indulging in a little hedonism.

She wrapped herself in a thick white terry-cloth robe, allowing herself to savor the feel of it against her bare skin before tying it tightly at the waist, despite the fact that her father was thumping his fist against the door again. She glanced at herself in the mirror and ran her fingers through her short crop of dark hair, thinking with wry amusement of the reaction her new "do" was going to get from dear old dad.

She walked quickly to the door and opened it just in time to see her father's fist raised for one more fierce onslaught of knocking.

"Good grief, Dad. I heard you the first time," she told him teasingly. When he just stared at her, his fist still raised, she grabbed the lapel of his European-made suit jacket and yanked on it till he took the two steps required to cross the threshold and enter her apartment. She closed the door behind him and turned around.

"Good Lord, Lex, what have you done to your hair? Your *beautiful* hair?"

Alex tugged self-consciously at the short tendrils that curved around her neck. "I cut it, Dad. It was impossible to take care of it. It was constantly dirty or falling in my face…or serving as a breeding ground for a community of small insects. Besides, I like it this way. Don't you?"

By the look of abject regret on his face, Alex's father did not like it that way. "It was halfway down your back, Lex. So thick and shiny and beautiful. Just like your mother's used to be."

There was the crux of the problem, thought Alex,

instantly forgiving her father for his honesty. With short hair, she looked less like her mother.

"Do I get a hug or what?" she asked him.

Her dad pulled her against his broad chest and gave her a long, hard hug. He smelled like he always did, like most rich men did, she supposed—a cross between an expensive tailor's shop and a bank—wool and leather, a silver money clip full of crisp hundred-dollar bills and a dab of spicy aftershave. But he was her dad underneath the tycoon's façade, and she knew he must have had a hell of a time over the past two months since Richard's death.

She whispered against his cool cheek, "I'm so sorry I couldn't be here for the funeral. I know how hard everything must have been for you."

Her father released her and turned around immediately to walk into the living room, where her three suitcases still stood in a row in the middle of the floor. He spoke with his back turned to her. "It's still hard, Lex."

She nodded, although he couldn't see her, and said, "I'm sure it will be for a long time. You don't get over something like that that easily, or that soon." She took a step closer and awkwardly added, "You probably think, since there was no love lost between me and Richard, that I don't know what I'm talking about, but when Mom died I thought my world had ended."

He turned and smiled crookedly, sadly. "But, ironically, that's when my world expanded to include you. I'll always be grateful to Sasha for telling you who your father was before she died. And I'll always be grateful that she raised you to be such a beautiful, wonderful young woman."

Alex felt her eyes well with tears and blinked them away. Her mother had passed away ten years ago from cancer, but she still got misty whenever she and her dad talked about her. They both got misty.

Too bad her half brother, Richard, had never managed to feel the tiniest bit sympathetic or sentimental about the brief but intense love affair his father had had with a young Russian immigrant art student twenty-six years ago when he was in between his first and second wives, resulting in a little girl he never even knew he'd fathered till she showed up on his doorstep at the age of fifteen.

Richard had been jealous of Alex from the beginning, had accused her of only being after the old man's money, and had had no compunction about frequently calling her a bastard to her face and behind her back. Richard had never had a good relationship with his father, but Alex's arrival on the scene had worsened it.

Alex had hoped his marriage to Karlie—a sweet girl, from what she could tell from their infrequent encounters at strained family functions—would soften Richard, mature him. But that hadn't happened. Even the three little girls he and Karlie had had together hadn't cured Richard of his selfish arrogance.

Alex felt a stab of guilt for thinking ill of the dead, but truth was truth. Richard wasn't a very nice man. In fact, she felt a lot sorrier about poor Karlie getting killed and being denied the pleasure of raising her three girls—to whom she was devoted—than she did about her own brother's passing.

"I don't suppose you've got a thing to drink in

this place?'' her father asked suddenly, looking around her dusty apartment.

"Just liquor," Alex answered. She grinned. "It keeps, you know, whereas juice and milk and all that healthy stuff tend to rot over time."

Her father nodded curtly. "Liquor will do."

Alex's smile faltered. "At ten in the morning, Dad? Drinking's not going to bring Richard back."

He sat down on the couch with a sigh and patted the cushion beside him. "No, but it's not Richard I'm trying to get back."

Alex frowned and took a seat beside him on the sofa. "What are you talking about?"

"We haven't talked since the accident. Something has happened. There was a surprise at the reading of Richard's and Karlie's wills."

This eased, rather than intensified Alex's concerns. "Is this about money? Because if it is, may I remind you that you'll always have more money than you'll ever need and—"

"It's not about money, Lex. It's about the girls."

"The girls? You mean Richard and Karlie's little girls?"

"Exactly."

"Don't tell me they gave the girls to Karlie's parents! Those two acted like they were on some kind of hallucinogenic drug half the time, if you ask me. I can't believe Richard would give guardianship of the girls to those wackos just to spite you, Dad!"

"He didn't."

Alex pressed a hand to her chest. "Whew! You had me worried for a minute. So what's the problem?"

"The problem is, Richard and Karlie gave the girls to someone else."

"Someone else? Who?"

"Someone I had never even heard of till the lawyers called me and told me to expect this guy at the reading of the will. I was worried that Richard had given away half of the Ethington assets. Now I only wish that were the case."

Alex caught and squeezed her father's hand. "Oh, Dad. I had no idea...."

"The girls are far more valuable to me than any amount of money, Lex. Richard's and Karlie's deaths really hit me hard and made me realize how precious children are, how important the family is. Hell, Richard and I hadn't exchanged a civil word in over three years! That's a horrible legacy to live with. I'm getting on in years, Lex, and I want to spend the time I have left with you, the only child I have left, and my grandchildren...making memories, not money."

Alex nodded sympathetically. "So, who is this man they gave the girls to?"

"He's a doctor in New Hampshire named Spencer Jones."

"Is he married?"

"No."

Alex shook her head, perplexed. "Why did they choose *him?* Is he a friend of Richard's?"

"No."

"What's the connection, then?"

"I had him checked out and found out that he's an old boyfriend of Karlie's. In fact, he's the guy she ditched the night before their wedding to run off with Richard."

"Oh…I didn't know anything about that." Alex thought for a moment, then said, "Well, if he's a nice guy, maybe that explains why Karlie wanted him to raise the girls, but that doesn't explain why Richard would agree to such a plan. In fact, knowing Richard, I could more readily believe that, as an old boyfriend of Karlie's, this Dr. Jones fellow would be the last man on earth he'd want raising his children. It just doesn't make sense."

Her father sighed again and shook his head sadly. "It's a mystery, all right. And it's killing me, Lex. I wasn't there when you were growing up, and I blew it with Richard."

"Oh, Dad…" Alex wouldn't say so, but she didn't think any man could have been a father to Richard without somehow "blowing it."

"I just want a chance to be there for those girls, to be to them what I never was to you and your brother. I'm doing everything I legally can to get them back, but my lawyers say it looks pretty grim. I'm contesting the will, but that won't keep the adoption proceedings from going forward unless I can—"

"He's already started adoption proceedings?"

"Yes. He's not wasting any time, that's for sure."

Alex narrowed her eyes. "I assume the girls have hefty trust funds. Do you think he's after their money?"

"I don't know. I only saw the guy once, at the reading of the will, and I was seeing so much red at the time I didn't even pay much attention to what he looked like, much less have the presence of mind to try to judge the man's character."

"Judging a man's character is pretty hard to do

unless you spend a substantial amount of time in his company—see him at work, with friends, with family.''

''If I showed up in Jonesville to observe, I'm sure Dr. Jones would waste no time in getting a restraining order against me.'' Her father smiled weakly. ''He's somehow got the impression I'm unreasonable, impatient and volatile.''

She patted his hand and said wryly, ''No doubt he got that impression at the reading of the will. I assume you ranted and raved and thumped that huge fist of yours against the table a time or two.''

His smile broadened, became more genuine. ''You know me so well.''

''And love you so well, despite your being unreasonable, impatient and volatile at times. Too bad you don't let more people see your soft side.'' She gave his hand a last squeeze and stood up, saying briskly, ''So what kind of liquor do you want, Daddy? I'll indulge you this once, but then we're going to put our heads together and figure out what to do about this dilemma.''

''Make that whiskey on the rocks, sweetheart.'' As she was turning to go, he added, ''Thanks, Lex. I'm glad you're home. I just wish you'd give up this crazy profession of yours and stick around town— hell, just stick around the western hemisphere— longer than two weeks at a time. You certainly don't need the money with the trust fund I gave you. Maybe if I added another million…?''

Alex rested her hands on her hips. ''Speaking of millions, that's about how many times we've gone over this. You know I love what I do, and I'd do it no matter how much money you stashed away for me.''

''But why do you have to go to such godforsaken places?'' he complained. ''Places so damned backward and dirty and dismal you have to live like a vagrant and...and cut your beautiful long hair to keep the lice at bay?''

''Because I like to see the way other people live, Dad. To see and experience different cultures, to see what means 'home' to them. And to capture that all on film for everyone else to see, too. Besides, I like a challenge. I won't get that sitting on my fanny in a Boston high rise, up to my neck in luxury.''

He shook his head, then grinned reluctantly. ''Despite all that, I love you, anyway.''

She grinned back. ''Even with shorn locks?''

''I'd love you if you were bald and tattooed, Lex...but don't get any ideas, okay? Now where's my whiskey, you scalped little globe-trotter?''

A WEEK LATER, Richard Ethington the Second was no closer to getting his granddaughters back. And, adding to his aggravation, Alex had been called away on another assignment...something for a nature magazine. Or so she allowed her father to believe.

Alex was actually on a little assignment of her own, the purpose of which she was keeping a secret. She'd prepared for this assignment, and thrilled her father in the process, by actually spending some of the money he'd stashed away for her. She'd bought a new Subaru four-wheeler—and was driving it up the Kancamagus Highway through the most breathtaking Autumn foliage she'd ever seen, toward

Jonesville, located in the famously beautiful north country near the White Mountains of New Hampshire.

Since it was the third week of October, when the thick forests of maple trees, beeches, birch and oak had reached their peaks of vibrant red, orange and gold, Alex shared the road with tons of tourists. All the extra people would be gone in a few days, as soon as the trees had lost the last of their leaves and before the frigid New Hampshire winter set in. She was relieved when she was finally able to leave the main highway and drive along another road headed northwest.

After miles of bumping bumpers with what felt like half the population of North America, this road seemed almost deserted. Alex passed through valleys surrounded by rolling hills of pine and cedar, their dark green interspersed with the brilliant colors of the deciduous trees as they followed the slope of the land, sometimes to the very edge of the road. Small farms, houses old and new, and white church spires on village greens dotted the countryside. Every New England picture postcard Alex had ever seen appeared tantalizingly before her photographer's eye and thrilled her soul.

Why, she wondered, had it never occurred to her to take pictures of places and people in nearby New Hampshire? She'd been to China, Russia, India and South America, never considering for a moment that a local culture might be just as interesting. Time would tell. This trip would serve a twofold purpose. She'd discover and record everything she could about New Hampshire and its people—which was going to be her cover, anyway—and discover everything about Dr. Spencer Jones at the same time.

She used her mother's surname professionally, publishing her photos and articles under Alex Koskov, so that would shield her real identity from Jones. And, if she was successful enough in this little mission to actually see her nieces, they'd never recognize her. Although the two women had gotten along just fine, Richard had discouraged Karlie from socializing with Alex. Added to the problem was Alex's hectic work schedule and the three-year feud between Richard and their father, so it was no wonder that Alex hadn't seen her nieces since the oldest, Elizabeth, was two, and the second to the oldest, Margaret, just a baby. Camilla Rose, who would turn a year old later that month, she'd never set eyes on.

Yes, it would be easy to remain incognito. She doubted that anyone, much less Spencer Jones, had any inkling that Richard Ethington the Third even had a half sister. He had certainly never advertised the fact.

She'd get as close as possible to Jones and his family and learn what she could. If he was a decent man, worthy of raising her nieces, she could at least reassure her father and herself about that, knowing that, for the time being, at least, the girls were in good hands.

But she firmly believed that her father was just as worthy and capable of raising the girls as this Dr. Jones might be—not to mention it made more sense—and she was determined to figure out a way to make that happen.

She'd been racking her brain to come up with a

plausible reason for Jones to take on the raising of three strange children when he was fully aware that the paternal grandfather of those children was dying to do it himself. Were the trust funds his motivation for suddenly wanting to become a bachelor daddy?

If not the trust funds, what else could it be? Could he have been carrying a torch for Karlie all these years? Did he have some misplaced feeling of obligation to his deceased ex-girlfriend? Her father had told her Karlie had left a letter for Jones....

But, whatever his motivation, Alex was going to find out what it was—good or bad—and hopefully use it to their advantage. She had nothing against Spencer Jones, but his emotional investment in those children couldn't even come close to what her father was feeling.

When the sign for Jonesville, population 1,289, popped up alongside the road, Alex turned off the highway and found herself on Main Street, where Jones's office was located. A large banner hung over the street, announcing a Harvest Day's Festival for the upcoming weekend. It was two o'clock on a sunny Friday afternoon, and she figured Jones would still be seeing patients. She drove slowly down the street, peering through the windshield at the addresses and storefronts.

There it was! The building had a plain brick façade, but the glass-fronted door was covered with a life-size Frankenstein monster poster, and the large front window was draped in orange crepe paper and decorated with various sizes of handmade paper pumpkins, each with a different face. Alex was a little surprised by the festive look, and wondered if her nieces had helped with the decorating.

She looked for a parking spot and finally found one two blocks away. Before getting out of the car, she pulled down the mirror on the back of the sun visor and examined her reflection. Although cutting off her long hair had been much more traumatic for her than she'd let on to her father, she was getting used to the short cut. Without the length pulling it down, it waved on its own, giving her a rather carefree, stylish cap of curls.

Her burgundy lipstick complemented her olive complexion, and she'd actually taken the time to add mascara and a thin line of smoky eyeliner to her large gray-green eyes, something she hardly ever did while on assignment or slumming around the apartment and neighborhood. In a cranberry-red sweater and gray slacks, she looked like the average New Englander on holiday or running errands, she decided, and stepped out of the car with confidence.

Watch out, Dr. Jones, she thought, *'cause here I come!*

When Alex entered the doctor's office a bell tinkled overhead and a dozen people in a tiny waiting room turned to look at her. Suddenly her confidence wavered. She was a stranger here, just as much as she was in China or India or Iran. But, for some reason, these inquiring eyes discomposed her more than all the others had. Maybe it was because rural New Englanders were reputed to be conservative, close-knit and suspicious of outsiders. Or maybe because it had never been more important for her to somehow "fit in."

But rural New Englanders couldn't be *that* unfriendly because one of them suddenly waved a black crocheted handbag in the air and called out to her, "Over here, honey! There's a seat right over here by me!"

Alex looked at the elderly woman attached to the waving handbag, smiled politely and headed for the seat beside her. She noticed that the silver-haired, petite woman's feet dangled several inches above the floor and realized that she was sitting on a thick cushion covered in a bright, sunflower-splashed fabric that looked decidedly incongruous against the conservative black of the woman's dress. The woman also wore black gloves and pumps and a small velvet pillbox hat. In her dated, somber clothes, she looked like a widow, but her brightly rouged cheeks and big smile seemed to indicate otherwise.

"I don't believe I've seen you around these parts," the woman observed as soon as Alex sat down. "My name is Myra Henderson. What's yours?"

"I'm Alex Koskov."

"But isn't that a man's name?"

"It's short for Alexandra."

"Oh. Well, my goodness. Say, did you buy the old Martindale house? No, you couldn't have. I'd have heard about you from Hattie Levine. She works at the Jonesville Department of Utilities. She knows whenever power or water's turned off or on."

Alex continued to smile politely. "I suppose that would clue her in to who's coming and going."

"So, what are *you* doing? Coming or going?"

"I'm just passing through. Actually I'm from Boston."

"Are you sick, or did you just run out of birth control pills while you were out gadding about?"

Alex nearly choked. "I beg your pardon?"

Myra looked coy. "I know how you young people are."

Alex couldn't help but laugh. This lady was confusing her generation with another. But even if she had been a leftover free-love proponent from the sixties or seventies, it wouldn't be anyone's business but her own.

She glanced around the room to see if the rest of Dr. Jones's patients looked, or were acting, as quirky as this one. They all seemed pretty normal, grown-ups and children alike, and some even gave her a sympathetic smile as if they understood what, or should she say whom, she was having to deal with.

She also noticed that, from inside the office, the pumpkins on the windows had names on the backs of them. Some of the handwriting obviously belonged to children—there was Josh, Heather, Zach, Amanda—but other signatures looked definitely grown-up. Alex's eyes narrowed. The grown-up signatures were all *female* names. There was Carrie, Amy, Janet, Cheri....

Myra tapped her on the shoulder. "You'd better check in with Velma," she advised Alex. "Whether you're here because you're sick or whether you're here for birth control pills, it doesn't matter. Velma always wants to know who's here, what's wrong with you and whether or not you've got insurance. That's her job."

Alex figured Velma was the receptionist whose blurred silhouette she could see moving behind a wavy glass window set in the wall, with a little shelf in front of it, at the far end of the room. She stood up and walked to the window and waited until a plump woman with a black beehive hairdo opened it and inquired in a businesslike tone, "Yes? Can I help you?"

"I was wondering if it would be possible to get in to see Dr. Jones today." She was also wondering if Velma's hairdo was part of an Elvira getup in keeping with the decor, but didn't dare ask. Velma was the person who would determine whether or not she'd get past the waiting room and into the examination room.

Alex had been practicing a cough in the car on the way up and she tried it out now. *Cough, cough.* "I'm just passing through, but I started feeling sick this morning and it's just getting worse. I know I don't have an appointment, but I'm willing to wait."

Velma's black, fantastically arched eyebrows lifted. She eyed Lex suspiciously. "You're not using false pretenses to see Dr. Jones for some *other* reason, are you?"

Alex swallowed hard against a throat that had gone chalk-dry. Could this woman possibly know...? "I beg your pardon?" she rasped.

"You're not another nanny wanna-be, are you? Because, if you are, you're just wasting your time. Due to the underhanded shenanigans of young women vying for the position, Dr. Jones has decided not to hire a nanny at all." Velma sniffed officiously. "And when and *if* he decides to resume his search for a nanny, he's got more than enough applications on file from every young woman between here and Dixville Notch!"

Alex was relieved and intrigued at the same time. "I'm afraid I don't have the slightest idea what you're talking about. I'm not a nanny. I'm a photographer. I just want the doctor to check my throat." *Cough, cough.*

"Your throat does sound a little rough," Velma conceded reluctantly, her brows knitting. She stared at Alex for a few seconds, then reverted to her businesslike tone. "There's a flu going around in Lancaster. I'll fit you in...sooner than later. Don't want you spreading your germs around the office. Do you have insurance?"

"I'll pay cash for the visit."

"Very well." She handed her a metal clipboard with a form attached to it. "Fill this out, please."

While still standing at the window, Alex did as she was instructed, then scooted the clipboard across the shelf toward Velma.

"Thank you, Ms.—" she looked at the form "—Koskov. You may return to your seat. It'll be a few minutes. And please cover your mouth when you cough."

Alex obediently covered her mouth and coughed...three times, for good measure. She sat down again by Mrs. Henderson and while the elderly woman prattled on, mostly about her colorful cushion and why she needed it, Alex thought about Velma's scolding diatribe about young women resorting to "underhanded shenanigans" just to win the position of nanny to her nieces. As Alex saw it, there were two possible explanations for such behavior. Either word had got about that the girls were filthy rich, or the unmarried Dr. Jones was a Brad Pitt look-alike and therefore a babe-magnet.

But, beyond this, Alex was worried that the girls might not be getting the kind of quality child care they should be getting. Her father had told her that Jones's grandmother was seventy-five. Three little girls would be a handful even for someone fifty years younger!

As Alex chewed her lip and worried, nodding her head and making the appropriate sounds required to keep up her end of the conversation with Myra Henderson, the bell above the door tinkled again, announcing the arrival of more patients for Dr. Jones. Alex looked around, wondering where they'd sit in the packed-to-capacity room, when she suddenly realized that the new arrivals could be none other than the doctor's grandmother and Alex's three little nieces! Talk about luck! Myra immediately confirmed her suspicions.

"Well, bless me, if it isn't Irma Jones and those three little ladies the doctor inherited from that Karlie Thompson girl he courted in high school." She leaned close to Alex's ear. "The baby's a sweet thing…likes everyone. But those two older girls are kind of snooty…like their real pa, I hear. Dr. Jones has had 'em for more than two months now, but neither Elizabeth nor Margaret will speak a word to him!"

Alarmed by Myra's revelations, Alex studied the new arrivals closely. Irma Jones, a short, trim, gray-haired lady in jeans and a pink sweatshirt with kittens appliquèd on the front, looked more like sixty-five than seventy-five. Alex assumed she was there to see her grandson, but as she was greeted and engaged in conversation by people on both sides of the waiting room, her progress toward his office was slow. She didn't seem to mind, though. She was pleasant and smiling and cheerful.

Camilla Rose was in a stroller...and, oh, what a cutie she was! She had a tumble of dark curls and big, bright blue eyes. Everyone smiled and cooed at her and she smiled right back, flapping her arms and making gurgling, happy sounds. Dressed for the cool weather in pink corduroy overalls and a white pullover, she looked anything but neglected. Alex had to restrain herself from walking right over, picking her up and giving her a big squeeze!

Elizabeth and Margaret were another matter altogether. Elizabeth, the oldest, was almost a replica of her mother with her reddish-gold pigtails, blue eyes and small, refined features, while dark-haired Margaret and Camilla obviously took after Richard. The older girls were dressed very neatly and girlishly in green jumpers and white tights, with matching green bows in their hair and black Mary Jane shoes on their dainty feet. Again, neither appeared neglected...except that they looked as sober as undertakers, not once cracking even the smallest of smiles!

Elizabeth and Margaret responded politely to direct questions, but seemed to be trying to ignore the friendly interest of the people surrounding them. They kept their heads together, whispered a lot to each other, and looked...well, as Myra had put it...*snooty.*

Alex thought this might be the girls' way of handling the trauma of losing their parents and suddenly being transplanted into a totally strange and new environment. Or, worse case scenario, Richard might have taught the girls to think of themselves as better than everyone...certainly better than these very ordinary, surprisingly friendly small-town New Englanders.

Either explanation for their behavior was distressing to Alex. Her heart went out to them. Richard might not have been the best of brothers, but these little girls were her own flesh and blood! She was more determined than ever to make sure the girls were returned to the Ethington fold where her father would welcome them with joy and warmth.

Her father and Richard might not have gotten along, but he'd been a wonderful and loving father to her and could be just as wonderful and loving a grandfather to Richard's children. That he hadn't been given the chance, that these girls had really been taken away from their own blood relatives and were now showing signs of maladjustment to their new home and "Daddy," was fueling Alex's growing indignation.

"Well, how are my four favorite females?"

Alex's head snapped up when she heard the doctor's voice at close proximity after hearing the deep, pleasant murmur of it through the closed door separating the waiting room from the examination rooms and office. He was standing right beside her chair, smiling down at the three little girls and his grandmother from the vantage point of about six feet four inches of lean, muscular male.

Alex stared up at Dr. Spencer Jones and immediately understood why women from Jonesville to Dixville Notch were suddenly hankering to be nannies.

Chapter Three

"We're fine, Spence," Irma said, bending her head back at an almost painful angle to return her tall grandson's smile. "Aren't we, girls?"

"Yes, Gran," the two older girls answered promptly and politely, almost in unison, but Alex noticed that neither of them looked at Dr. Jones or smiled. Camilla, on the other hand, was holding out her chubby arms to him and shouting an ecstatic and unintelligible welcome in baby talk.

He bent to pick her up, tucked her against his chest and kissed the top of her curly head—a sight that would easily send a lovelorn nanny into rapturous swoons—then returned his gaze to the older sisters, who seemed determined not to make eye contact with their court-appointed guardian, no matter what. "Well, girls, what have you been doing since Lizzie got out of school?" he asked pleasantly.

So the good doctor called Richard Ethington the Third's oldest child *Lizzie,* eh? Alex knew that her half brother had insisted on no nicknames for the girls.

Elizabeth and Margaret remained silent, seeming to draw courage and resolution from each other by standing closer and linking arms. When it was obvious they weren't going to reply, Irma laid her hand on Elizabeth's shoulder and said, "Elizabeth had her first piano lesson with Mrs. Pringle and we all went along to listen. I thought she did wonderfully. Didn't you think so, too, Margaret?"

Alex watched—the whole roomful of townspeople watched—as Margaret's eyes lifted ever so briefly to meet Dr. Jones's hopeful expression. She might even have made a reply that implied his inclusion in the conversation if Elizabeth hadn't bumped her shoulder and whispered something in her ear.

"Yes, Gran," Margaret finally answered in a very sweet and respectful tone. "Elizabeth did a very good job. But, please, could you tell Dr. Jones that her name is *not* Lizzie?"

Being chastised in front of a roomful of people by a four-year-old would be embarrassing for anyone, no matter how politely it was done, but Alex got the impression that Jones was more disappointed than embarrassed. In fact, she was quite sure she detected a fleeting expression of hurt cross his features before he forced another smile—a wistful one—and said, "She just looks like a Lizzie to me. I'm sorry, Elizabeth. I'll try to remember that you don't like nicknames."

Elizabeth gave no indication that she'd heard the doctor's apology and Alex—along with, probably, everyone else in the room—couldn't help but feel sorry for him. But she shook off the urge to sympathize and told herself that he'd brought this problem on himself by taking the girls away from the bosom of their real family.

Irma's determinedly cheerful voice broke the tension. "Camilla's getting a new tooth, Spence. I thought I'd drop by and pick up some of that gel that numbs it before she starts fussing."

"This one fuss?" Jones teased as he gently pinched Camilla's dimpled chin. "I don't believe it."

Irma gave a wry chuckle. "It's rare, but it happens. Just never around you."

"I'll get the gel for the baby, Dr. Jones," Velma announced briskly as she bustled her way into the crowd. "And I'll put Mrs. Henderson in Room One while you look over her chart."

She held out the thick manilla folder to Dr. Jones, forcing him to give Camilla back to Irma. It was obvious that she was trying to get her boss back on the job, although no one in the room seemed to be irritated by the family stopping by and taking the doctor's time. They were probably fascinated by the little soap opera being played out in full view of everyone, hoping, like devoted TV viewers of the genre, that the hero would win the heart of the heroine...or in this case the *heroines*...and they'd live happily ever after.

But Alex couldn't feel that way. As nice a guy as Dr. Jones so far appeared to be, he couldn't be any nicer or more appropriate in the role of "Daddy" than her father was. And, in her opinion, Elizabeth and Margaret's refusal to give him the time of day proved that this arrangement simply wasn't working. Why Karlie and Richard had thought it would work in the first place was absolutely baffling!

"Ms. Koskov? Follow me and the doctor will see you after he's seen Mrs. Henderson."

Alex was startled to suddenly be spoken to and downright disappointed that she couldn't stay and watch the doctor say goodbye to her nieces. She'd have to see and hear a lot more before she could make a truly accurate assessment of the situation. She just hoped her plan to wiggle her way into their lives would work, because she needed as much eye-witness evidence as she could get to convince the authorities that the girls would be better off with their natural grandfather.

Along with Myra Henderson, who slid off her cushion carefully and tucked the colorful accessory under her arm, Alex followed Velma through the door and into the back, which consisted of just two examination rooms, Velma's cubicle and Dr. Jones's private office at the rear.

"See, I told you they didn't talk to him," Myra whispered loudly to Alex just before she was motioned into Room One by Velma, who was looking none-too-pleased by Myra's gossiping.

"They talk to Irma. I think they even *like* her—they call her Gran, you know—but they don't talk to *him* at all."

"The doctor will be with you in a minute," Velma snapped, then closed the door in Myra's face just as she was about to say something else to Alex. "Come with me, Ms. Koskov."

Alex was escorted to the next room where Velma briskly patted the papered top of the examination table. "Hop up here, Ms. Koskov. The doctor will tell you if you need to take off your clothes."

"Thanks for the warning," Alex murmured as the door closed behind Velma, but the idea of taking her clothes off for Spencer Jones had actually sobered her considerably. Not that she wasn't already as sober as a churchmouse. Seeing her nieces again and feeling a strong sympathy for their situation was more difficult than she'd thought it would be. She was sorrier than ever for her father, too, and the very idea that he'd be denied raising those beautiful little girls was more than she could stand!

But back to the taking her clothes off thing... She wasn't normally a shy or retiring person. During her many trips around the world she'd frequently lived in primitive conditions that were hardly private or conducive to modesty. Traveling with other photographers and journalists, Peace Corp and Red Cross personnel, she'd had to be pragmatic about where and when she could bathe and change clothes. It hadn't bothered her in those situations, and she'd likewise have to admit that no previous doctor's visits where the removal of her clothes was required had bothered her in the least.

Spencer Jones was undeniably attractive, but so were many of the men she'd traveled with. And so was her gynecologist, Dr. Mather. So...why did the idea of shedding her clothes for Dr. Jones make her "goose bumpy" from head to toe?

Part of her plan was to charm Jones, to use blatant flirtation to help her get access to the girls and his living arrangements. But she hadn't expected the complication of actually being *attracted* to him!

Scolding herself for her schoolgirl reaction to this man—who, she reminded herself, was the enemy— Alex slid onto the examination table and swung her legs back and forth, scowling and looking around the immaculate room in hopes of spying a magazine that would take her mind off the situation and help her relax. She didn't want the doctor to sense her hostility *or* her attraction. She had a part to play, after all, and—

Alex was startled when the door suddenly opened and Spencer Jones walked in. She'd been told that Myra Henderson was first on the docket and was prepared to wait several minutes. She wasn't ready for this…for *him*. At closer proximity, he looked even better, and the effect of those sky-blue eyes looking straight at her was like a mule kick to the head. She could feel her goose bumps growing to the size of land mines.

"Hello, Ms. Koskov. I understand you've got a cough."

"What are you doing here?" she blurted out.

He looked surprised, then laughed, the corners of his eyes crinkling attractively. "I work here."

Alex blushed. She never blushed. So why now? "I'm sorry. I…I just expected to be waiting longer. I was told that you were seeing Mrs. Henderson first."

He nodded, his eyes twinkling with amusement. "Believe me, if I'd seen Mrs. Henderson first, you *would* have been waiting a long time. She likes to talk."

"Er…yes, I know."

"I reversed the order because I was sure your visit would take less time. And since you're just passing through…" He picked up his stethoscope and rubbed it against the palm of his hand, then leaned forward and pressed it to her chest, just inside the V-neck of her sweater. He smelled like aftershave, breath mints and antiseptic hand soap. "So, I gather you became acquainted with Mrs. Henderson in the waiting room?''

''Y-yes. She's very friendly.''

He relocated the stethoscope a couple of inches to the left. ''Just breathe normally.''

She was trying to!

''Mrs. Henderson is friendly all right,'' he continued, ''and as nosy as a raccoon. I hope she didn't ask you a lot of personal questions?''

She stared at the front of his light denim shirt, at the hint of a hard chest behind it. That's when she first noticed his tie, too, wondering how she could have missed it before. It was covered with large, goofy-looking bats cavorting against a fluorescent orange background.

Alex decided that it was certainly a testimony to the attractiveness of a man when his personal charms could catch and keep a woman's attention long before she noticed a traffic-stopping tie! She swallowed with difficulty and finally answered his question. ''Well, does asking me if I'm here for birth control pills count as personal?''

He laughed again, letting his stethoscope fall. She watched his Adam's apple bob up and down, fascinated. ''In my book, it does.'' He took a step closer to the table and pressed his fingers to the underside of her jaw. ''But since we know you're here for a cough and a sore throat, maybe we'd better check your lymph nodes.''

Check whatever you want, Doctor, she fantasized saying. Alex's eyes drifted shut while Spencer Jones gently prodded her neck. His fingers were warm and firm.

''They feel fine,'' he murmured. ''No swelling.''

"That's…that's good, isn't it?"

"Yes." He pressed his hand to her forehead. "Your heartrate's a bit fast.… Been feverish?"

Not till now. "No. I don't think so."

"Open."

Alex knew her throat would look perfectly normal and she was beginning to worry that he'd realize she was faking it, so when the tongue depressor came out, she fell into a fit of coughing till her eyes watered.

He stood back and watched her for a few seconds, then filled a small cup with water at the sink and handed it to her. She croaked a thank-you rather convincingly, she thought, and drank the water.

"Since there are no signs of infection, I think your sore throat and dry cough is probably an allergy, Ms. Koskov. Velma tells me you're from Boston. It's likely you're reacting to something local, perhaps some weed or pollen in our New Hampshire woods. What I recommend is allergy medication—" he scooped a prescription pad from a deep pocket in his lab coat and smiled "—or to get out of town as fast as you can."

Alex realized she was about to be dismissed. It was now or never. "Well, I guess I'll need the allergy medicine then because I'll be in town for several days."

"Oh?" His eyes flicked up from the pad he was writing on. Did she detect a smidgen of interest in his expression, or was it just wishful thinking? "Visiting someone?"

Since she was definitely attracted to Spencer Jones, Alex thought it should be easy to flirt with him, but somehow her attraction made it harder. It made her jittery and uncharacteristically shy. But "shy" wasn't going to get her anywhere, so she crossed her legs and propped her hands on the edge of the examination table, creating a rather provocative pose that forced her shoulders up and her breasts out...what there was of them. She was no Pamela Anderson.

"No, I'm a photographer and I'm taking pictures for a nature magazine. Jonesville is a perfect location for me to work from. I plan to take lots of pictures in the woods just outside of town. Unfortunately there's no hotel here, and I'm afraid I'm going to be forced to drive in from Lancaster every morning. All that extra driving is going to take a precious chunk out of my workday."

He nodded thoughtfully. He wasn't writing anymore, so she'd got his full attention. She dropped one shoulder, tilted her head to the side and said, "Unless you can recommend a local bed-and-breakfast, or someone trustworthy that takes in occasional boarders?"

He was still watching her, his brows slightly lowered. She hoped he wasn't getting suspicious, but there was no way he could connect her with the Ethingtons...was there? But what else would he be suspicious about?

"Are you sure you're a photographer, Ms. Koskov?"

Alex suddenly realized that he was simply worried that she might be another "nanny wanna-be." Relieved, she performed a carefree laugh. "Rest assured, Dr. Jones, I'm not here looking for a position working under you...er...*for you* as a nanny." She felt her face and chest flood with warmth, but she forged on.

"Velma already interrogated me about that. I'm definitely a photographer with credentials that can be checked easily through the internet, and I have lots of pictures to take. *Do* you know somewhere I might stay for a few days? It doesn't have to be fancy. I'll be gone most of the day, anyway, and wouldn't be any trouble. It would really help me out."

Spencer wasn't sure why, but for some reason he did want to help Ms. Koskov. It wasn't because she was pretty, although she *was* pretty ...*damned* pretty, in an alluring, exotic way he wasn't used to seeing in the rural realms of New Hampshire.

And it wasn't because she was flirting with him...although she was doing a damned good job of that, too. He was always scrupulously professional with his patients. While within the hallowed confines of his office—and especially his examination rooms—he never thought of women in any romantic or sexual context at all. It was usually very easy to do. But not today. Today, he had to admit, he was having trouble thinking of this woman as anything but distractingly attractive.

Once she left the office, however, and since she wouldn't be his patient on any sort of continuing basis, maybe it would be okay if he...if they....

What was he thinking? He'd been dating Bernice Galloway, Lizzie's kindergarten teacher, for four months now and, by an unspoken but assumed mutual agreement, they hadn't been seeing anyone else. They hadn't slept together, mostly because Spencer wasn't in love with her—at least, not yet—and he was pretty sure she wasn't in love with him, either. And since Bernice wasn't the type of female you just dallied with, he'd kept his libido firmly in check.

The thing was, maybe it had been a little *too* easy to keep his libido in check. Such would not have been the case if he'd been dating for four months the exotic woman presently sitting on his examination table. In fact, he had a hunch he wouldn't have lasted four days...or maybe even four *hours* in a relationship situation with Ms. Koskov without wanting to make passionate love to her.

But, despite the fact that Spencer wasn't feeling any particular fireworks with Bernice, he was fond of her, thought she was a good person who would make a good wife and mother someday, and he was willing to go along at a leisurely pace and see what happened. So far, things between them had been going well.

Sure, "going well" seemed like a rather tame way to describe a romantic relationship, but it fit his life right now. His main concern were his girls. The last two and a half months had been incredible— incredibly difficult and incredibly wonderful. Being made guardian of three little girls was the biggest surprise and challenge of his life, but it also had become the most important thing in his life. He just wished...

Ah, hell, he knew—and Gran preached—that he needed patience, but it was hard as the dickens waiting for Lizzie and Maggie to talk to him, and seemed like an almost impossible dream that they'd ever call him Daddy.

"Dr. Jones?"

Spencer recalled his wandering thoughts. "Sorry, Ms. Koskov. I was thinking."

"About my predicament, I hope." She smiled, her even white teeth glinting between full, cranberry-tinted lips. "I'll bet you know everyone in Jonesville, and which ones take in boarders."

She was right about that. He knew two or three families that occasionally took in boarders, including his grandmother. But Gran wasn't looking for boarders these days. With her new baby-sitting job, she had plenty to keep her busy…at least during the day while he worked. But Ms. Koskov—he glanced down at her chart, Ms. *Alexandra* Koskov—would be gone all day taking pictures and his sociable grandmother would probably welcome some company at night in that big old house.

Alexandra… She sure had a pretty name. It sounded as exotic as she looked. It fit her perfectly. So why, as the chart indicated, did she choose to go by the much less feminine nickname of Alex? He generally liked nicknames, but in this case he'd choose the longer version any day.

Alexandra…

What harm would it do? he wondered, as his gaze rested on Alexandra's face, then flitted quickly and involuntarily over her slim curves. Why shouldn't he set her up with Gran? He'd probably be doing them both a favor.

Who's kidding whom? his conscience inquired sarcastically. He was probably just hoping that by setting her up at his grandmother's he might bump into her now and then. But even if he did bump into her, it wasn't like he couldn't control himself….

"You must be thinking again," Alexandra suggested with a coy, enchanting smile. "Wanna share?"

Spencer's stomach did a flip-flop and his heart started hammering. Patients had flirted with him before, but he'd never before reacted like a hormone-riddled teenager. It was alarming, disconcerting, *unprofessional*. He wanted this conversation over with and this alluring woman out of his examination room as quickly as possible. Maybe that's why he decided to make her the offer.

Maybe.

He finished writing the prescription—in his haste, managing to make it more illegible than usual—and stood up. Without smiling and in a businesslike tone, he said, "I'll ask my grandmother if she'd be interested in putting you up for a few days, Ms. Koskov."

Her eyes widened. "Oh, does your grandmother take in boarders?"

He nodded curtly. "Sometimes. But she's pretty busy these days taking care of my three girls and I can't guarantee she'll agree to the idea. I'll have to call and ask her." He handed her the prescription.

She took the paper, glanced at it briefly, then looked up at him. Her eyes were a beautiful gray-green, something he hadn't noticed before, even when he'd been examining her. "So when will you know?"

"Give me an hour or so to fit a phone call in between patients. If my grandmother can't do it, I'll have Velma check with some other families in the area who take in boarders. When you come back, Velma will have the address and information for you at the window." He extended his hand and smiled tightly. "It was nice meeting you, Ms. Koskov. I'm relatively sure the medication I prescribed will help your throat, and I hope you get some great pictures for your magazine."

Looking uncertain and a little rushed, Alexandra took Spencer's hand and asked, "But if I stay with your grandmother, won't I see you now and then?"

Spencer registered, but tried desperately to ignore, the jolt of awareness that shot up his arm when his large hand wrapped around Alexandra's much more delicate fingers. What was it about her that made him want to melt like putty on a hot sidewalk? "Possibly, but not likely. I keep pretty busy at night. Dinner, stories, baths and bedtime for three little girls takes up most of the evening. And you *did* say you'd be gone all day most days, didn't you? Otherwise, your staying at my grandmother's might not work out."

"Oh, yes," she assured him quickly. "That's definitely what I said. I promise I won't be any trouble at all to her during the day."

He suddenly realized he was still holding her hand and dropped it like a hot potato. "Well… then…that's fine. Check with Velma later. Goodbye, Ms. Koskov."

"Goodbye, Dr. Jones," he heard her say to his back as he hurried out the door as if he had a dying patient in the next room instead of a simple case of hemorrhoids. He closed the door behind him and headed to his office. He needed a breather before facing Myra Henderson. She was basically a sweet, harmless old lady that he'd actually grown rather fond of over the last five years, but he had a feeling he wasn't up to her usual barrage of personal questions. He felt exposed and vulnerable after finding himself so taken by a woman he'd only known ten minutes.

"Taken" was an understatement. He was hot for her. He smiled wryly, imagining the word Lust branded on his forehead for all the world to see.

"Doctor?"

Spencer turned, sure he was blushing guiltily. "Er...yes, Velma?" She was staring at him oddly. Maybe he really did have Lust branded on his forehead. He gave it a surreptitious swipe.

"Are you ready to see Mrs. Henderson?"

"Er...yes. Do you have her chart?"

"It's in your hand, Doctor."

He laughed. "So it is. Guess I was daydreaming a little."

Velma raised a kohl-penciled brow. "With a roomful of patients left to see, I'd say daydreaming is the last thing you should be doing, Dr. Jones."

Spencer nodded like a chastened schoolboy. "You're so right, Velma," he agreed soberly as he headed down the hall to Room One. "Daydreaming is the last thing I should be doing."

Especially, he told himself, over some woman who was just passing through town. He certainly didn't need a distraction like her in his already way too complicated life. He'd set her up at his grandmother's—after all, he'd said he would—but he'd make very sure he stayed out of her way. With all his girls to take care of—including Bernice—he'd have plenty to keep him busy, anyway.

There was really nothing to worry about.

Everything would work out just fine.

In fact, he foresaw no problem whatsoever with

Alexandra Koskov hanging around town for a few days...even if she was spending her nights right next door at his grandmother's.

But if he believed all that, why was his heart still beating like a first-time skydiver's about to jump out of a plane?

ALEX WAS WAITING ACROSS the street in the shadow of a large, brilliantly red maple tree when she saw Velma leave the office. Barring the remote possibility that Spencer had exited by a rear door—the building didn't appear to have a back alley to park a car in, and, besides, she knew he walked to work and lived just down the street—the doctor was still inside. She had been told to check with Velma, but she had no intention of getting the directions to her temporary living quarters from anyone but Spencer Jones.

She glanced at her watch. It was almost six forty-five and dusk was settling over the little town of Jonesville. Long shadows stretched across the street and golden remnants of sunshine reflected off the pumpkin-covered window of the deserted office. Deserted, that is, except for Spencer, who was obviously a dedicated doctor. As admirable as that was, it didn't, however, make him a good daddy. In fact, it might actually make it harder for him to be a good daddy.

Just as Alex had hoped and planned, moments later, Spencer walked out of the front door alone. He was minus his lab coat, wearing instead a dark green barn-style jacket with a denim collar. As he turned to lock the door, she ran across the street and was right behind him when he turned around.

"Oh, Dr. Jones!" She pressed her splayed hand against her chest and heaved a labored breath. "I almost missed you! Is Velma gone already?"

Spencer looked surprised, then flustered and a little irritated. "I told you to come back in an hour, Ms. Koskov. Yes, Velma's gone. We thought maybe you'd decided to stay in Lancaster after all."

"No, of course not." She gestured to the shoulder-strap case that held her camera. "It's just that I decided to take a few pictures and time got away from me. What did your grandmother say? Do I have a place to stay? I want to stay in Jonesville more than ever. Your woods are *so* beautiful!"

Did she imagine it, or was Spencer trying to suppress a grudging smile?

Alex had been aware earlier of Spencer's change of attitude in the examination room from his friendly, professional bedside manner to cool and businesslike. She'd chalked this up to his determination to abstain from flirting with a patient and respected him for it, but she was worried that he might be so concerned about drawing the proper lines between doctor and patient that he wouldn't call his grandmother after all. Staying with someone else in town wouldn't work out nearly as well as staying in the same house where the girls were baby-sat, but she'd manage, if she had to, to somehow wheedle her way into their family circle.

"Our woods are always beautiful, but especially in Autumn," Spencer finally conceded. "I've lost track of time myself when wandering around in them this time of year."

"Good, then you forgive me! So what about your grandmother?"

He chuckled. "She said yes."

"Wonderful!"

"She likes company and she was intrigued by your profession, Ms. Koskov. In fact, she's familiar with your work. She'll probably ask you a lot of questions."

"That's fine by me. But please don't be so formal, Dr. Jones. Call me Alex."

His smile disappeared. She saw something flash in his eyes, then he gave a curt little nod. He might have just agreed to call her Alex, but he hadn't asked her to call him "Spence," or even "Spencer." But Alex was nothing if not determined.

"So where does your grandmother live?"

He lifted his chin, motioning with his head. "Just up the street a little ways. Right next door to me."

"Oh, really? So we'll be neighbors." As if she didn't already know that, and plenty of other facts about Spencer and his family…thanks to her father's inquiries.

There was the curt nod again. "Yes, but I'm sure, with our busy schedules, we won't be bumping into each other very often."

She said nothing, but thought, *That's what you think.*

He looked around. "Where did you park your car?"

"Across the street. Shall I drive us both…um… home?"

She saw that flash of emotion in his eyes again. She couldn't be sure, but it looked a little like panic. "No. No, I like to walk home. It's a short distance, but it allows me to stretch my legs and generally get the kinks out. I like the fresh air, too. Clears the

brain…'' He stopped suddenly and gave her an uncertain look. "I can give you my grandmother's address and tell you exactly how to get there. Nothing
could be easier."

"I can think of something a lot easier," she said
with a smile. "I'll walk with you to your grandmother's, then walk back later to get my car. You
said it's only a couple of blocks, right?"

He nodded slowly. "Well, er…*four* blocks to be
exact." His brows knitted as if he were trying to
think of a logical reason to refuse her company for
a paltry four blocks.

Alex was amused and irritated at the same time.
She was beginning to wonder if Spencer's desire to
be professional was the only thing making him so
suddenly uptight around her. Then it occurred to her
that the reason he was skittish might be because he
had a serious relationship going on with some
woman…although her father hadn't mentioned digging up that bit of information about him.

But, after all, he was a healthy, good-looking
man. He was securely settled in his home and practice, thirty-two years old, and the instant daddy of
three little girls. The idea was disconcerting, disap-
pointing, but entirely logical that he could already
have a steady girlfriend…a steady girlfriend who
just might not appreciate another woman hanging
around the good doctor and his adorable charges.

Alex had a sudden vision of Spencer squiring
around some small-town sweetie, kind of like TV's
Andy Griffith courtin' Opie's teacher, Helen. They'd
dine and dance in Mount Pilot, then return to May-
berry for the guitar serenades on the porch, complete
with lemonade or buttermilk to drink with a plateful

of Aunt Bea's oatmeal cookies. She saw it all...the whole corny shebang.

But if she thought it was corny, why was Alex suddenly so jealous? She was only trying to get close to Spencer Jones for the girls' sake, right?

Alex realized that Spencer was gazing at her with an odd expression on his face. She must have looked as if she'd been temporarily transported to some other planet. "What are we waiting for, then?" she chirped, as if the last two minutes hadn't passed without her uttering a word. She started walking in the direction Spencer had been going before she'd waylaid him. Although he still looked a bit bemused, he fell in step beside her.

"I'm sure you're eager to get home to those little girls I heard so much about at your office. I saw them when your grandmother brought them by and they're really beautiful children. Tell me, Dr. Jones, how does it feel to be an instant father?"

"Well, I—"

"Spence! Oh, Spence!"

Alex and Spencer turned around and watched a pretty blonde head their way, carrying a canvas tote bag covered in a Noah's Ark motif. In tailored gray slacks, a black vest with bright red apples for pockets, and flat, functional shoes, she looked, to Alex, like an elementary schoolteacher. The only thing missing was the #2 pencil behind her ear and the chalk dust on her nose. Could it be...? Could she have been so dead-on when conjuring up a possible girlfriend for Spencer Jones?

"Who's that?" Alex asked bluntly.

"It's Bernice Galloway," he replied, then turned to look Alex squarely in the eye. "She's my..." He paused suddenly, blinked twice, then turned rather pink around the ears. "That is…she's Lizzie's kindergarten teacher."

Spencer could have kicked himself. Why couldn't he say it? Why hadn't he told the truth, the whole truth, and nothing but the truth? What was keeping him from telling Alexandra that Bernice was his girlfriend as well as Lizzie's kindergarten teacher?

But maybe it was simply because he didn't know *how* to say it….

In these modern days, a grown man didn't call a grown woman his "girlfriend," did he? "Significant Other" was politically correct, but sounded pretentious and absurd when spoken out loud. "Keepin' Company" and "Courtin'" were used only on black and white TV shows about small towns and sheriffs, and "She's my woman" was a little too macho.

Spencer suddenly realized that he'd never before had to introduce Bernice to anyone. Everyone in Jonesville knew her and knew they were dating. But was not knowing how to introduce her the real reason he was reluctant to tell Alexandra Koskov that Bernice was the other half of the couple everyone in town was betting would be engaged by Christmas?

He didn't think so.

And the real reason scared the hell out of him.

So maybe that's why he decided that the best course of action was to make absolutely certain there was no doubt in Alexandra Koskov's mind—and in *his* mind, too—that he was already taken. It was the honorable thing to do. The safe thing to do.

As soon as Bernice reached them, Spencer did

something he'd never done before. Right there on Main Street, in full view of every passing car and gawking pedestrian—and there were a few—he pulled Jonesville's kindergarten teacher into his arms and kissed her hard on the lips.

Chapter Four

The kiss was quick and, in Spencer's opinion, definitely lacking in finesse, but it left Bernice breathless and in an apparent state of shock. When he released her, he was immediately sorry he'd done something so impulsive. It wasn't fair to Bernice because it might make her think that he was ready to move their relationship to the next level. After all, he'd kissed her in public, as if declaring to the world—caveman style—that she was his and he was hers. He might as well have bonked her over the head with a club and dragged her off to the cave where she could sew them matching outfits out of animal skins!

That's certainly the way the people of Jonesville would interpret the situation—at least, all those who witnessed the kiss and all those who heard about it later. In other words, every single citizen of the town. And he'd put himself and Bernice in this damnable position solely because he wanted a certain flirtatious and alluring stranger in town to consider him off limits in the romance department.

But had it worked? While Bernice caught her breath and gathered her wits, Spencer slid a glance in Alexandra's direction. She was staring at Bernice, but he couldn't tell what she was thinking.

"Spence. My goodness...."

Now Spencer stared at Bernice. Her eyes were wide, her lips slightly parted, and she was pressing a hand to her chest. Then he watched with growing alarm as her expression changed from shy and embarrassed to flushed and pleased. The grin that inched up her cheek was coy.

Uh-oh.

Sidling up to him, she slipped her arm through his. "Well, I must say, I plan to accidentally run into you on the street more often."

Spencer chuckled uneasily. "Just a little kiss hello," he muttered.

She bumped her hip against him. "Makes me wonder how you'll say goodbye."

"Bernice, I don't think I've introduced you to Ms. Alex Koskov," Spencer said quickly, turning toward Alexandra. "She's a photographer and plans to be in town for a few days to take pictures for a nature magazine. She's staying at my grandmother's and I was walking her to the house."

Bernice wrenched her gaze away from Spencer and gave Alexandra a swift, appraising once-over. She couldn't help but notice how attractive Alexandra was but, perhaps since Spencer had just "marked" her as his with a public kiss, Bernice seemed disinclined to be jealous.

"No, you haven't introduced us," she said politely and with a gracious nod of her head as befitted a woman completely sure of herself and her man. "Pleased to meet you, Ms. Koskov."

Alexandra returned her smile. "Call me Alex. Pleased to meet you, too, Ms. Galloway."

"Oh, goodness, call me Bernice."

"Dr. Jones told me you're Elizabeth's kindergarten teacher, Bernice, but somehow I think you're a little more than that."

Bernice giggled. "Well, yes. Spence and I *do* date." She poked his chest with her forefinger and twisted it playfully, looking up at him through her lashes.

Spencer flicked another quick glance at Alexandra. Again, he was completely in the dark as to what she might be thinking.

"I'm glad to hear there's something more to your relationship than just being Elizabeth's teacher," Alexandra said, her lips still curved in a smile that seemed aimed for Bernice, but which suddenly slid teasingly in his direction. "After all, it would have been shocking—not to mention unhygienic—to learn that Dr. Jones greets *all* the teachers in Jonesville with a kiss on the mouth."

"Or anywhere else for that matter," Bernice joked back, then laughed and bumped her hip against him again.

Spencer was embarrassed and appalled. He'd had no idea that kissing Bernice on the street would make her so uncharacteristically giddy and flirtatious. She continued to hang on his arm, her gleaming eyes staring up at him as if she was a hungry mouse and he was a one-hundred-eighty-pound cheese mold.

"New Hampshire is a beautiful place," Alexandra finally remarked conversationally. "Especially in this neck of the woods."

"Yes, beautiful," Bernice agreed without taking her eyes off Spencer.

Watching Bernice bat her baby-blues at Spencer, Alex realized that there was no point in trying to converse with the woman any longer. She was clearly distracted. But who wouldn't be? Alex would probably be floating on the same cloud if Spencer Jones had planted a similar lip-lock on her kisser...and in full sight of all and sundry.

Judging by Bernice's surprised reaction, however, and Spencer's obvious discomfort, it wasn't something he did normally. That could only mean that he'd been deliberately advertising his more-than-friends status with Elizabeth's kindergarten teacher. For *her* benefit? Alex wondered.

Well, of course for her benefit, she immediately recognized. He was warning her to back off, either because he was sincerely smitten with his small-town sweetie or because, for any number of other reasons, he wasn't interested in acting on their attraction to each other. And she had a strong feeling he was as attracted to her as she was to him.

But wasn't that beside the point? she reminded herself. Her mission was to get close enough to Spencer and his grandmother to be able to spend time with and around her nieces. Actually, since she'd already managed to snag a room in his grandmother's house, more flirting was probably unnecessary. In fact, it might even be counterproductive. Maybe if she just treated him like a friend, he'd relax around her and she'd actually get better access to the girls. And by nixing the flirting now, it would spare her the possibility of getting involved with someone she only intended to double-cross in the end.

Ugh. Double-cross was such an awful word. She felt like a ruthless conniver, but what choice did she have? She was doing all this for a good cause—the reuniting of a family. And staying romantically uninvolved with Spencer Jones would spare them both some ugly scenes down the road, scenes that were bound to be ugly enough without the added complication of a fling between them.

Yes, Alex conceded, a girlfriend showing up on the scene was probably a godsend. So, why did she feel so damned disappointed?

Smiling politely, Alex discreetly turned and took a few steps away. She was determined to push aside her attraction to Spencer and refocus her eye on the real prize, the real reason for this trip to New Hampshire—getting the girls back to her father. She gazed across the street at the maple tree she'd been hiding under a few minutes ago and pretended to be giving Spencer and Bernice some privacy. She had excellent hearing, however, and was easily able to overhear their conversation.

"What did you want, Bernice?"

"Hmm?"

Alex couldn't see, but could easily imagine Bernice's continued besotted stare.

"Were you trying to catch up with me to tell me something?" he prompted. Did Alex detect a smidgen of irritation in his voice?

"Oh, yes! Yes, I did want to tell you something. I found a book on the internet that might help you with Elizabeth and Margaret! It's at the Baker Memorial Library at Dartmouth and I'm having them send it to the library at school. We have a lending system with them, you know. There are some interesting theories that might help you understand why the girls just don't seem to want to accept you, no matter what you do.''

Out of her peripheral vision, Alex thought she saw Spencer turn slightly and glance her way. ''That's great, Bernice, but maybe we should talk about this some other time.''

Alex wondered if Spencer just wanted to cut short his conversation with Bernice or if he didn't want Alex to overhear what she was saying about the girls. But didn't the whole town know that Elizabeth and Margaret weren't talking to him?

''Oh.''

That one cold syllable from Bernice held a wealth of meaning. Alex couldn't help a small, knowing smirk. Wasn't that just like a man? First he delights her with a kiss, then he offends her by cutting her off.

''I guess you want to go so you can take Ms. Koskov to your grandmother's,'' she said coolly. ''Will I still see you tomorrow at the fair?''

''Of course.'' His tone was conciliatory now. ''I'm sorry, Bernice. I don't mean to rush you. And I'm really grateful for any help you can give me concerning the girls. It's just that it's late and I need to get home.''

She was instantly understanding. ''Of course, the girls are waiting for you. That's okay, Spence. You run along home now.'' There was a pause, then, demurely, ''Aren't you going to kiss me goodbye?''

Alex couldn't help but glance over at them. She had to see if he was going to kiss Bernice goodbye like he'd kissed her hello. Of course it didn't really matter whether he kissed her or how he kissed her because she'd already made up her mind to nix the flirting thing, but it was interesting that this time he only gave her a peck on the check.

"Goodbye, Bernice."

"Goodbye, Spence." Her tone was deflated. "Oh, and goodbye, Ms. Koskov…er…Alex," she called as a polite afterthought. "I hope you get some good pictures."

Alex turned to wave and smile. "Goodbye. Maybe I'll see you around town."

Bernice's smile wavered. Clearly she'd rather not see Alex around town, particularly since after that peck on the check she wasn't as sure of her man as she was before. Throwing Spencer one last brittle smile, she turned and walked away.

When Spencer joined Alex and they began to walk again in the direction of his grandmother's, he seemed sober and preoccupied. She wasn't sure what to say or whether it would be welcome if she spoke at all, so Alex kept quiet as they traversed the two blocks that constituted the rest of Jonesville's business district north of Spencer's office, all of the stores closing or closed for the night and hardly another pedestrian on the sidewalk.

Since Spencer was still silently brooding by the time they'd reached the residential area where his grandmother lived, she simply took in the charm of the street as they strolled along, admiring the big Victorian houses with their gingerbread details, the carved pumpkins on the porches and the yellow and red leaves from the bordering trees strewn on the otherwise tidy lawns.

Dusk was upon them and lights shone golden in Halloween-decorated windows. Delicious dinner smells wafted from kitchens. A mother standing on her front porch waved at Spencer, then called her children home. As the two little boys ran past, their cheeks glowing pink with exercise, Alex couldn't resist taking out her camera and snapping a couple of shots.

When Alex lowered her camera, she found Spencer looking at her curiously. "I thought you were a nature photographer."

"No, I'm a photographer currently on an assignment to take pictures for a nature magazine," she corrected, meeting his frown with a sunny smile. "I take pictures of everything…everyone. In fact, I prefer taking pictures of people over any other kind of photography I do. Pictures are so revealing, don't you think?"

He nodded slowly, still frowning.

"For example, if I took a picture of you right now, it would reveal that you're upset about something. It's not your girlfriend, is it?"

He acted surprised, then alarmed that she would remark on his mood. He seemed to shake himself and force a smile, then a bit of false bravado. "Oh, no, there's nothing about Bernice upsetting me. Things with me and Bernice couldn't be going better."

"Well, good," Alex said, taking on her new "friend" role with enthusiasm. "I'm glad to hear that. She seems very nice."

"Oh, yes. Bernice is *very* nice. In fact, she couldn't be nicer."

"Does Elizabeth like her?"

"Yes, Elizabeth likes her." The sigh and the returning frown that followed seemed to say, *I'm the one Elizabeth doesn't like.*

Alex forced away the surge of sympathy she felt for him. She couldn't afford sympathy. "So I gather, from the huge banner over Main Street that there's a Harvest Days Festival tomorrow."

Spencer's furrowed brow cleared slightly. "Yes. It's an annual event here in Jonesville. As well as being traditional and lots of fun, it's a great money-raiser for several charity organizations and school projects."

"I've never been to a Harvest Festival. What do you do?"

As well as fishing for an invitation, Alex was genuinely curious. Spencer studied her for a minute, then shifted his gaze to straight ahead.

"We meet on the town square where booths and tents are set up. There's everything from pumpkin pie eating contests, best blueberry jam contests, pumpkin carving contests, fortune-telling, craft fairs and—speaking of unhygienic—a kissing booth." He turned to smile at her for the first time since the short but fascinating Bernice interlude. Her gaze drifted from his eyes to his lips. Much against her will, Alex warmed inside.

"You're right, it does sound fun," she murmured. Then, forcing herself to look away from the doctor's finely molded kisser, added, "I...um...love pumpkin pie."

"You're in luck, then. Gran baked pumpkin pies last night. You're sure to be offered a slice for dessert tonight."

But she'd rather be offered an invitation to tag along with him and his family to the festival.

"So, are you going to the festival?"

"Everyone goes. I'm surprised the word hasn't gotten out that all of Jonesville is virtually unprotected while the townsfolk make merry at the fall festival. We could be cleaned out by vandals in a matter of minutes."

"I suppose the girls are looking forward to it?"

"You bet. Gran has been working on their costumes with them for weeks now. There's a Halloween costume contest...actually two of them. One for children and one for adults."

"What are you going as?"

His grin was spontaneous and boyish. "Like everyone else, you'll just have to wait and see."

She jumped on the suggestion while pretending innocent surprise. "Oh, so you think I ought to take an hour or two off from my picture-taking tomorrow and go to the festival?"

There was an awkward and telling pause, then he said, "Sure, if you think you can spare the time. And...don't worry about being alone. You'll make friends quickly enough."

Still no invitation, but Alex couldn't blame him. They were attracted to each other and he had a girlfriend. He was just trying to stay out of trouble. But she wanted to spend the day with him and the girls tomorrow, to see them interact. On Monday he'd be back in the office all day. How was she going to manage to finagle some time with Spencer and her nieces if the good doctor was determined to be so darned honorable?

Suddenly she got an idea. Maybe if she convinced

him that she had a boyfriend, Spencer wouldn't consider her such a threat. Maybe he'd even convince himself that she hadn't been flirting with him in the first place, but was just being friendly.

Quickly she concocted in her mind a romantic hero. He'd be handsome and rich, of course. Perhaps European...someone she'd met during her many trips abroad, with a sexy accent and a fancy name. Heck, if she was going to make up a man, why not make him everything a girl could want? And by introducing the topic of rich versus not-so-rich, maybe she'd get a feeling for Spencer's own attitudes toward money and find out whether or not the girls' trust funds were in jeopardy.

Another brainstorm... He wouldn't be just her boyfriend, he'd be her fiancé! That ought to make Spencer feel safe around her.

She sighed pensively. "I wish *Dimitri* were here. He'd love this town. And I'm sure he'd get a big kick out of a country fair."

Spencer stopped in the middle of the sidewalk and turned to look down at her. "Dimitri?" he repeated. "Sounds Russian, like your name. Is he your brother?"

"Dimitri's my fiancé."

Alex couldn't deny that she was flattered by Spencer's look of stunned dismay. He recovered quickly, however, and asked, "So, why can't he be here? He works, I suppose."

Alex laughed. "I'm sure he does. He *says* he does. But most of his business is done on a cell phone in between tennis matches. He comes from a wealthy family and basically handles the finances so profits keep coming in on a regular basis. He's in

Paris right now meeting with some business associates.''

Spencer raised a brow. ''Paris? I no longer wonder why he's not here. I wonder why you're not *there*.''

She shrugged. ''I have a job to do.''

''With a rich fiancé, do you have to work?''

''I want to work. I love what I do.''

''Will you still do it after you're married?''

''Of course.''

''What if Dimitri doesn't want you to?''

''We've already settled that. My job is part of the package.''

Spencer smiled another of those brilliant smiles that made Alex's knees go weak. Damn, why'd they do that?

''I'm impressed, Alex,'' he said with an apparent sincerity that made her feel even weaker in the knees. ''It's always refreshing to meet someone who doesn't think money is the be-all and end-all of everything.''

So…did that mean he couldn't care less that Elizabeth, Margaret and Camilla Rose were richer than rocky road ice cream with fudge sauce and whipped cream on top?

Spencer resumed walking and said nothing more till he stopped in front of a large slate-blue Victorian house with white trim on all its bric-a-brac and turrets. The yard was bordered with flowers—mostly chrysanthemums and marigolds this late in the season—and plants hung from the rafters of the wraparound porch. This house had its share of Halloween decor, too, from the carved pumpkins on the porch steps, to the cardboard cutouts of black cats, flying witches and ghosts taped to the windows. There were even orange lights flickering in the short, round bushes that lined the sidewalk leading up the house.

"Your grandmother's house is charming," Alex said, meaning it. And it appeared to be an ideal place for little girls to spend their days. Now she'd just have to see what went on *inside* the house.

Spencer opened the gate and waved Alexandra through. As she walked to the house ahead of him, he admired the view and decided that this woman would look good from any angle. When she'd told her fiancé that he'd have to take the whole package or not at all, the man would have been a fool to say no...because she was one helluva package. Not only was she sexy and smart, but she also appeared to have a great work ethic and attitude about what was important in life. Spencer hated to admit it, but he envied the hell out of this "Dimitri" fellow.

So, why had she flirted with him before? he wondered as he watched her hips subtly sway as she walked up the steps to the porch. But maybe she hadn't been flirting with him. Maybe he was reading more into those smoldering glances and alluring shoulder rolls than she'd intended. Maybe that's just the way a woman named Alexandra Koskov behaved around *all* men. Maybe it was part of her personality.

Maybe.

At the door, Spencer reached past her and turned the knob.

"It's not locked?" Alexandra asked, surprised.

"Not necessary in Jonesville." Spencer pushed the door open, then cupped her elbow and guided her inside. Even that minimal contact sent his blood racing.

The entry hall was lit, as usual, by the hurricane lamp on the table at the bottom of the stairs. Down the hall, light from the kitchen in the back of the house spilled onto the glossy hardwood floor.

"Spence, you're home!" exclaimed Gran as she appeared at the door to the kitchen, balancing Camilla on one hip. "'Bout time. Camilla's been fussing for the last half hour. She knows when you're past due."

At the sight of Camilla kicking her legs and reaching for him, a big smile plumping her cheeks into shiny apples, Spencer no longer envied anyone. To have this little girl take so much delight in his company was a source of happiness he'd never imagined before.

"Put her on the floor, Gran. Let her crawl to me."

"There you go, sweetie." Gran set Camilla on the floor, but held onto her hands while Camilla stood straight and tall in the high-topped shoes they'd just bought for her last weekend. "Go to Daddy."

Spencer got down on one knee and held out his arms. He glanced up at Alexandra to brag, "Watch this. You've never seen a kid move so fast. She's got Olympic Gold Medal runner written all over her."

But instead of going immediately down on her hands and knees when Gran released her, Camilla remained standing within the circle of Gran's hovering hands. Grinning like a little lunatic, she wobbled a bit, then took a single step forward. Spencer's heart skipped a beat.

"Heavens to Betsy," Gran breathed excitedly. "I think she means to walk to you, Spence."

"Has she ever walked before?" Alexandra asked.

"Just around the furniture, holding on to whatever she could grab," Spencer answered. Camilla's smile was a little hesitant now and she was standing very still. She obviously sensed the excited tension in the air and was probably nervous about taking the next step. Still holding out his arms to her, Spencer smiled and spoke soothingly. "It's okay, sweetheart. You're doing great! Come on over to Daddy. Walking or crawling, it doesn't matter to me. Do what feels good to you, Camilla."

The corners of Camilla's mouth curved toward the ceiling again. She took another step...then another. Spencer kept up reassuring eye contact with her, but he also noticed two small figures appear in the background, standing behind and to the side of Gran. Lizzie and Maggie were watching from the kitchen doorway.

Camilla was so excited by her first steps, she was flapping her arms and making gleeful noises. Spencer was afraid she was going to throw herself off balance. But that was expected. She'd fall down and get up a million times in the process of growing and learning. That was normal. That was life. But if Camilla was only doing what was expected, what every normal child learned to do, why did he have such a big lump in his throat?

"What am I standing here for?" Gran exclaimed. "I'm getting the video camera!"

Gran disappeared into the kitchen, but Spencer didn't think she'd have time to get the video camera before Camilla had either made it into his arms or

plopped down on her fanny. Suddenly a flash illu-
minated the hallway, then another. Alexandra was
taking pictures.

Startled at first by the flashes, Camilla paused and
swayed. She blinked once or twice, then caught
sight of Spence again and took another step. Six
more steps taken in a rush and with her arms flapping wildly, Camilla finally made it into his waiting
embrace. He stood up and tossed her in the air, making her squeal and giggle. Then he bounced her
around the entryway in a victory dance.

"You did it, Camilla Rose! You walked!"

He turned and looked exultantly at Gran, who had
just returned, out of breath, with the video camera.
"Keep it up, Spence. I didn't get the walking, but
the dancing's pretty good stuff, too."

But Spencer couldn't keep dancing. He suddenly
felt far from exultant. Shifting his gaze to the
kitchen doorway, his heart had plummeted. Lizzie
was staring at him as if he'd just bombed Disney-
land.

Maggie's expression was different...more confused than anything, her big blue eyes round with
indecision and anxiety. It appeared as though she
wanted to smile and be happy about Camilla's first
steps, but she kept looking to her big sister for a cue
to know how to feel, how to act.

Lizzie's repressed anger and the influence of it on
Maggie was stealing the joy out of their lives. *All*
of their lives. If only she'd talk to him...scream at
him, even. Anything was better than her continued
condemning silence.

"Elizabeth, is there something you want to say to
me?" Spencer asked her quietly.

She said nothing. She didn't move a muscle. She just continued to stare at him, but not with the same overt hostility. Whenever she realized her feelings were showing—good or bad—she quickly shuttered them behind a cold reserve.

Everyone else stood frozen, too, watching and waiting like Dodge City citizens caught on the street in the middle of a showdown. He remembered for a fleeting moment that Alexandra was in the room, a stranger witnessing their domestic troubles, but he couldn't be bothered with anything as trivial as embarrassment.

"You seem angry with me, Elizabeth" he persisted. "Would you like to tell me what's wrong? I'll listen to every word. And I promise I won't get mad at you, no matter what you say."

Still Lizzie didn't speak, didn't move. It was almost as if she were in a trance. But there was something in Lizzie's expression that made Spencer hope. For a second or two he thought he detected a tiny flicker of hesitancy in those china-blue eyes. Eyes that looked so much like Karlie's... Maybe she wanted to give in, to finally end this silent rebellion against him.

But a single cautious step in her direction changed everything. Suddenly she turned and looked at Gran. Gravely she announced, "Gran, we mashed the potatoes, just like you said. Shouldn't we eat before everything gets cold?"

Spencer silently cursed himself. He'd blown it. The chance had passed.

"I think we'd better say hello to our guest first," Gran answered in her usual steady and cheerful tone. Without Gran, Spencer wasn't sure what he'd do.

She was a rock. Spencer just wished he had half as much patience and faith as she did. *She* was sure that Lizzie would come around. *He* wasn't so sure.

Gran passed him and held out her hand to Alexandra. "You must be the very talented Ms. Koskov. I've seen some of your work, most notably in *National Geographic*. Please come into the kitchen and sit down while the girls and I finish up dinner. We can chat and get to know one another. Would you like some tea?"

"Tea would be lovely. And, please, call me Alex."

Feeling all sorts of emotions she hadn't even begun to sort out, Alex followed Irma Jones into her warm and delicious-smelling kitchen. Preceding Spencer—who was trying very hard not to look disappointed—she saw that Elizabeth had already climbed onto a stool by the counter and was taking some dishes out of the cupboard, handing them one by one to Margaret. Both girls looked curiously at Alex, and when Gran introduced her, they both stopped what they were doing and said in very ladylike tones, "Pleased to meet you."

"Pleased to meet you, too," Alex answered with a smile. She was hoping the girls would be more receptive to someone they'd met on their own turf and wouldn't be as aloof as they'd been at the office. When they smiled shyly back, Alex's hopes seemed justified.

Along with hope, two other emotions immediately crowded in. First, regret. Regret that, because she'd seen so little of her nieces over the years, they didn't have a clue who she was.

And guilt. Guilt because they smiled and talked

to her, a perfect stranger, but wouldn't utter a single word to Spencer.

But Alex pushed aside the guilt by reminding herself that because of Spencer Jones, her father had missed Camilla's first steps.

"Why don't you sit down and I'll make that tea," Irma said, unaware that she was harboring a spy. Damn, there was that guilt thing again.

Alex smiled at the older woman. "I'd appreciate the tea, Irma. And I'd rather help these girls set the table than sit down, if that's okay."

Behind their carefully controlled expressions, Alex saw Elizabeth's and Margaret's eyes light up. Already she was making headway.

Chapter Five

Spencer watched, fascinated and jealous, as Alexandra became friends with his two oldest daughters in the time it took to eat dinner. They'd warmed to a few other people—Gran and Bernice, for example—but never so quickly. And he couldn't help but wonder if it was because Alexandra wasn't from Jonesville, wasn't part of their new life. She exuded an unconscious glamour that was probably more like the women they'd gotten used to in the rich circles her parents had moved in.

But no, upon consideration he realized that that probably wasn't true. From things Lizzie and Maggie told Gran, he'd concluded that the girls had spent most of their time with nannies. They'd loved their parents—well, at least it was apparent that they'd loved Karlie—but Karlie and Richard took frequent trips and were often gone two or three weeks at a stretch. And Karlie and Richard's social life had been busy, taking them away most nights of the week when they were at home in Boston.

As for the nannies, apparently they came and went like ice-cream flavors of the month. Lizzie had explained once to Gran that "Daddy never liked our nannies. At first he would, but pretty soon he always sent them away.''

''Spence?''

Spencer was recalled by Gran's voice. He realized he'd been lost in thought again. Embarrassed, he snatched a glance at Alexandra. She'd seen him preoccupied more often than not in their short acquaintance. But she wasn't looking at him. She was looking at Lizzie, listening to his daughter explain the difficulties of stretching her small fingers from *C* to *E* for her first piano lesson that afternoon. The green-eyed monster reared its ugly head again.

''Hon, I asked if you wanted more mashed potatoes and gravy,'' Gran prompted.

Spencer roused himself, threw his napkin to the table and sat back in his chair. ''No. No, thanks, Gran. Everything was delicious, but I'm full, and I need to get the girls home and into bed pretty soon. They've got a big day tomorrow.'' He looked at Camilla in the high chair next to him, nodding over her half-full plate of food, her hands, face and a lock of hair over her right ear coated with mashed potatoes, and peas scattered everywhere within a two-foot radius. ''Looks like Camilla's taken a hit from the sandman already.''

Alexandra laughed. ''She looks adorable.''

''She won't look adorable in the morning if I don't get her in the bath and get that stuff washed out before she goes to bed.'' He smiled wryly. ''Believe me, I know this from experience.''

Alexandra laughed again, then turned to Irma with a smile. ''The dinner really was delicious. We all thought so.'' She turned to Lizzie and Maggie. ''Didn't we, girls?''

They nodded enthusiastically.

"And you helped make it! I have to confess, I *still* don't know how to mash potatoes. But then, I don't get much of an opportunity to cook in my line of work. At least not in a normal kitchen. I *did* open a few cans of baked beans on my last trip to China and heated them up over a propane burner."

Lizzie and Maggie gazed at her, beguiled. "Did you have to eat the beans with chopsticks?" Maggie wanted to know.

Everyone laughed, even Spencer. The mental image was quite entertaining. "No, thank goodness. We did take along some American eating utensils. And it's a good thing, too, because I can't eat beans without dropping them down the front of me even when I use a spoon!"

The girls were delighted by this confession. Who wouldn't be? Alexandra was a charming mix of sophistication and the-girl-next-door. You could admire her and relate to her at the same time.

"Let's get busy, girls, and clear the table," Spencer said, more abruptly than he'd intended, the scrape of his chair on the hardwood floor rousing Camilla from sleepy contemplation of her own reflection in the metal high chair tray.

He tried to ignore the irritated looks Lizzie and Maggie threw him. They obviously didn't want to leave the fascinating company of their new friend…especially to go home with *him*.

"Spence, you go along," Gran told him as she, too, stood up. "I don't mind washing the dishes by myself."

"But you cooked dinner, Gran, and I don't feel right—"

"Oh, hush. Camilla's about to drop facefirst into her potatoes and peas. Go on home now." She gathered handfuls of silverware.

"Well—"

"I'll help Irma with the dishes," Alexandra volunteered, then stood up and immediately began to stack plates.

"All right, ladies. I know when I'm beat," Spencer conceded with a chuckle. He turned to pick up Camilla. "And this one must be beat, too, to be conking out an hour before her bedtime."

While he worked on getting a limp Camilla out of her high chair and Gran carted the silverware in an empty serving bowl into the kitchen, Spencer noticed that Lizzie had gotten up from the table and pulled Maggie to a corner of the room. She was whispering to her and Maggie was nodding, the two of them looking like a couple of pint-size coconspirators.

Now what? Spencer wondered. Having finally extracted Camilla from the chair, he held her against his shoulder, where she immediately snuggled against him and began to suck her thumb. He watched warily as Lizzie and Maggie ended their little conference and approached Gran, just returning from the kitchen.

"Gran, Margaret and I want to stay and help you and Alex clean up," Lizzie said. "Dr. Jones can take Camilla home and put her to bed, but we're not sleepy yet."

"That's not up to me to decide, girls," Gran hedged, darting a concerned look at Spencer. She knew how awful it made him feel every time the girls referred to him as "Dr. Jones."

"What about storytime?" Spencer asked them. "You know I like to read to all three of you at once. Camilla will be asleep soon—"

Lizzie turned to Alexandra. "Would you read to us, Alex? There are plenty of books here. After we're done with the dishes, you could read to us and then walk us home."

Alexandra's cheeks turned pink and her gaze flicked to Spencer, then flicked away. She was embarrassed and probably feeling sorry for him. Not usually concerned with how he appeared in the eyes of others, particularly where his girls were concerned, he had to admit he was getting pretty tired of being royally snubbed. That Lizzie and Maggie preferred the company of a stranger over him was bad enough, but that he was just as unwillingly charmed by Alexandra Koskov made it even worse.

Confused and frustrated, he spoke much more irritably than he intended. "Alex has been traveling all day and she hasn't been feeling well. Don't put her in a position where she feels she has to say yes to whatever you girls demand."

Spencer's tone of voice surprised them all. Gran, Alexandra, Lizzie and Maggie stared at him. Again the look in the girls' eyes made him feel as though he'd just blown to smithereens Tinkerbell and the whole Disney gang.

"I'm sorry," he said gruffly. "I didn't mean to grumble at you girls. It's just that I don't think tonight is a good night for staying up past your bedtime for *any* reason."

"He's right, girls," Alexandra said soothingly. "I'll read to you another night. Maybe tomorrow night, or Sunday."

"Do you promise?" Lizzie asked plaintively.

"I promise. Now, you'd better go home and get your sleep so you'll be rested up for the festival tomorrow."

Maggie tugged on the hem of Alexandra's sweater and looked up at her like an appealing puppy. "Will you be there, too?"

Alexandra nodded and playfully pinched Maggie's nose. "I plan to go for a little while. I'll look for you, okay?"

Maggie beamed. "Okay. See you tomorrow."

"Yeah, see you tomorrow," Lizzie echoed.

Gran stooped down and opened her arms. "Now give me a hug, girls, and say good-night," she ordered briskly.

Lizzie and Maggie did as she said, wrapped their arms around her neck and squeezed, then kissed her cheek. Oh, how Spencer wished they'd—just once!—throw those little arms around *his* neck and kiss *him* on the cheek. Their affection for Gran was real, too, not forced. And if Alexandra stuck around for any length of time, they'd probably be just as smitten with her. What was he…hamburger?

While Gran helped the girls gather their belongings and put on their jackets, Alexandra came up to him. Stroking Camilla's hair, she smiled and said, "Thanks, Spencer, for getting me a place to stay with your grandmother. I think it's going to work out just fine."

It was the first time she'd called him Spencer instead of Dr. Jones. The effect was unsettling. Also unsettling was the fact that she was standing close enough for him to smell her warm, womanly scent. Something musky, exotic, spicy-sweet. He watched her long, slim fingers sift through Maggie's short dark curls and imagined how they might feel in *his* hair.

"Good night, Alex," he said abruptly, turning away to pick up his coat from a nearby chair. "Maybe we'll see you tomorrow at the festival."

Or maybe not…please, God!

Kissing Gran on the way out, he never looked back.

ALEX WAS HEADED FOR the kitchen with a stack of dishes when Irma returned from walking Spencer and the girls to the door. A part of her was inwardly rejoicing in the fact that she and the girls had gotten along so well, and another part was feeling guilty. She tried to hide both emotions behind a friendly and nonchalant attitude.

"Wow, those are really sweet children. I'll bet they look adorable in their Halloween costumes. What are they dressing up as?"

"Oh, they're sweet all right," Irma said, somewhat tartly. "But not to everyone." She turned on the hot water, plugged the sink and swished in a capful of dish soap. "Don't get me wrong. I love the dickens out of 'em. But they can be hurtful."

Alex picked up a dish towel and draped it over her shoulder. There were other dishes to carry in from the dining room, but she wasn't going to miss an opportunity to talk with Irma about the tense situation between Spencer and her nieces.

"Well, I won't pretend I didn't notice something going on between your grandson and the two older girls. And I did hear something about it at the office today from Myra Henderson."

Irma's eyebrows rose as she donned rubber gloves. "Myra will gossip with anyone, friends and strangers alike. But she hasn't told you anything the whole town doesn't already know."

"That much I gathered," Alex said with a nod. "Spencer doesn't try to hide the fact that there's an adjustment problem going on between him and Elizabeth and Margaret."

"Lizzie, mostly. I mean...*Elizabeth*. Even I want to call her Lizzie." She dumped handfuls of silverware into the steaming water. "Elizabeth being so stubborn about it is pretty ironic...."

"Ironic? Why?"

Irma shrugged and, without answering the question, asked one of her own. "Do you know the story behind Spence getting the girls?"

"Just what Myra told me," she lied. "Just that some old girlfriend of Spencer's left the girls to him in her will. Didn't she and her husband die in a car accident or something?"

"It was a plane crash." She set to work on the silverware, energetically wiping them with the dishcloth, then placing them in the clean basin for rinsing. "It's been nearly three months ago that he picked those girls up at their fancy house in Boston and brought them here. The family was very rich."

"I see."

"For the most part, they've adjusted beautifully. The girls and I get along really well, Elizabeth's doing great in school and, as you can see, the baby adores Spence. The girls are pretty reserved around most people, taking their time to warm up, but I think that's partly because of the way they were raised before they got here, and partly because their worlds have been turned upside down recently and they're naturally a little shy and anxious." She peered over her bifocals at Alex. "But they sure took an instant shine to you."

Alex averted her gaze as she swung the faucet to her side of the sink, filling the basin with hot rinse water. "I like children. I made an effort to get to know them and they responded…much more quickly and warmly than I expected."

"I'll say!" Irma acknowledged. She cocked a brow and grinned. "Are you sure you don't want to give up your glamorous career as a world-famous photographer and be a nanny?"

"If I did, I'd be afraid to say so," Alex answered with a chuckle. "Velma made it very clear that because of 'underhanded shenanigans' on the part of smitten females wanting the job only to get close to your eligible grandson, he was no longer looking for a nanny. At first, she suspected me of being one of those underhanded females."

"Velma's very protective of Spencer. But, actually, *I* was the one who convinced him to put off the search for a nanny. He said he didn't want to take advantage of me, but heck, I'm their granny now and I enjoy having them around! And I wanted the girls to feel secure in their new home. Nannies come and go, but I'm not going anywhere for a while…God willing."

"Yes, it must be a huge adjustment for them. When I saw them at the office and heard their story from Myra, my heart went out to them." She looked up, adding quickly, "And to Spencer, too. It must be awful to be so completely rejected by the girls."

"I wouldn't say completely." Having finished

with the silverware, she scanned the countertop. "We need the glasses next."

Alex followed Irma into the dining room, where they gathered the glasses, then returned to the kitchen. "What do you mean, you wouldn't say 'completely'?"

Irma carefully submerged and washed a glass before answering. Alex rinsed and placed it on the drainboard. "I see them respond to him…in their eyes. Margaret especially. It's Elizabeth that's holding back and, at the same time, holding back Margaret. Elizabeth's the one that won't let herself love Spence…or won't let him know, or acknowledge to herself, that she loves him already."

Something in Alex's chest twisted painfully. "You really think she already loves Spencer?"

Irma smiled at the dishwater and said fondly, "Who wouldn't love Spence after a while? Especially when he's as good as he is to those girls? You should see how he reads to them, tucks them into bed."

I intend to, Alex thought.

"And without getting a lick of affection back! Except from Camilla, of course."

Alex couldn't resist asking. "So, why's he doing it? I heard—" Now she was really stretching the truth and probably getting Myra in trouble. "I heard from…er…Myra that the girls' grandfather wanted them."

Irma's quick look was surprised and irritated. "I didn't know that bit of information had got around. That wasn't something we told anyone." She pursed her lips, thinking. "But then, maybe Spence told Bernice. She's not usually a gabster, but she'd only have had to tell one other person to start the rumor mill.''

Alex chuckled uncomfortably. ''Well, who knows. Hey, maybe I just thought Myra told me that the grandfather wanted the girls.''

''No, she *must* have told you. He *did* want the girls. Still does. He's fighting Spence in court, tooth and nail.'' She was finished with the glasses and reached for the dishes, carefully sinking a stackful into the bubbly water. ''Don't know why he wants them, though. He never paid a bit of attention to them before his son died. I heard he hadn't set eyes on them for three years and had never even seen little Camilla Rose. Can you imagine? What kind of grandfather is that?''

Alex had to hold back the urge to heatedly defend her father. However, she couldn't resist suggesting an explanation for her father's absence of grandfatherly visits. ''Maybe the girls' father didn't allow the grandfather be a part of their lives. Maybe it wasn't his fault that he didn't see them for three years.'' She shrugged. ''And—who knows?— maybe he wishes he could make up for all that now.''

Irma peered at her over her bifocals again, her expression keenly curious. Alex was afraid maybe she'd gone too far.

''I suppose all that's possible,'' Irma conceded after a while. ''But, even if all that were true, Spence has his own reasons for wanting to respect Karlie's wishes and raise the girls as his.''

''That brings me back to my original question, Irma. Why *is* Spencer so determined to respect Karlie's wishes? Why would he take on such a respon-

sibility when the girls' grandfather is so willing—''
so desperate, she added to herself ''—to do it himself? After all, at least the Ethingtons are family.''

Irma shook her head with disgust. ''Myra knew
their family name, too? That was something else we
tried to keep quiet about. That Myra is some piece
of work.'' She turned to Alex. ''Have you heard of
the Ethingtons?''

Alex could have kicked herself for being so care-
less. She was getting too keyed up talking about this.
She needed to cool it. Finally she nodded, saying
casually, ''Sure. I've heard of them. I'm from Boston and they're one of the first families, aren't
they?''

''How about your family, Alex? Are you originally from Boston?''

Alex was relieved to be able to say, ''No, I'm
originally from New York. My mother was first generation Russian—''

''Was?''

''She died ten years ago.''

''I'm sorry.''

''Thank you. And my dad…. Well, I didn't meet
him till I was fifteen.'' She paused, then added,
''I'm the product of what was quite a passionate
love affair, I guess.''

Alex expected Irma to act a little shocked by this
confession, shocked and disapproving. But Irma surprised her by saying, ''Well, better you come from
a real love affair than from a loveless marriage.''

Alex smiled. ''I couldn't agree more, Irma.''

''I wish Spence held the same opinion. Him and
Bernice…I don't know.''

Alex was instantly alert. "What about Spence and Bernice?"

Irma shook her head. "Never mind. It's none of my business. Tell, me, Alex, what's your father like? Did you keep in touch after you finally met him?"

She was disappointed when Irma dropped the subject of Spence and Bernice, but she couldn't act too curious. "My dad's a great guy. And, yes, we keep in touch." She smiled again. "That is, we keep in touch between my assignments, which, as you know if you've followed some of my work in *National Geographic,* takes me all over the world."

This prompted further questions from Irma about Alex's work, which changed the topic of conversation entirely. Alex was well aware that Irma had dodged the question—again—as to why Spencer was so willing to take on the responsibility of raising the girls when their real grandfather wanted to, but she was prepared to be patient. As eager as she was to get to the bottom of this mystery, she knew she shouldn't push too hard, too fast, for information. Irma was smart. She'd figure something was fishy if Alex carped on Spencer and the girls all night.

When the dishes were finished, everything wiped down and what little leftovers there were put in sealed containers and stashed in the refrigerator, Irma brought up Spence and the girls on her own. Slipping off her rubber gloves and hanging them over a towel bar, she said, "You know, coming from a rich family like they did, I expected the girls to sit around and wait to be waited on. But they aren't like that...weren't like that even from the beginning. They're helpful and they want to learn. I was surprised that they already knew how to make a few baked sweets and such. Seems their mother liked to putter around in the kitchen with them...when she was around.''

''Do they miss her?'' Alex couldn't resist asking. ''Do they ever...you know...cry?''

''When they're around me, they sometimes mention her...sort of in passing, you know. Always sweet memories. Never anything said about her being mean or indifferent. But Spence says he's caught Elizabeth crying in bed a couple of times. Figures she's cried a few other times he hasn't seen. He wants to comfort her, but she won't let him. It's a darned shame.''

It *was* a shame. But wouldn't it have been easier for Elizabeth if she'd been able to at least stay in the same town she'd lived in with her mother? Stayed part of the same family she'd grown up around for the first five years of her life instead being shipped off to virtual strangers? Sure, Irma wasn't a stranger now, but Elizabeth seemed determined to keep Spencer in that category.

Irma took Alex upstairs next and showed her her bedroom. It was a lovely room furnished with heirlooms and a private bath with a big claw-foot tub.

''We added the bathroom. It used to be an oversize closet, quite a luxury back when the house was built. It's been nice to have for guests and family visiting.''

''It's beautiful. Everything I've seen of the house is beautiful,'' Alex said truthfully. She was a real sucker for anything Victorian.

''Would you like a tour of the rest of it?''

Would she!

An hour later, Alex had seen every inch of the

house and heard the abridged history of the Jones family, and was enthralled with both. And Irma was wonderful. The girls could certainly do worse in the granny department. If they lived with her dad, they wouldn't even have a granny. But Alex pushed aside that fact as unimportant. She'd never known *her* grandmother and she was getting along just fine, wasn't she?

"Well, I need to walk back to my car and drive it down here so I can unpack," she finally told Irma as they concluded their tour in the upstairs hallway.

"Oh, you left your car in town?"

"Right across the street from Spencer's office. I—"

But Alex was interrupted by the sound of the front door opening and slamming shut, then Spencer calling out, "Gran? Gran, where are you?"

"Up here, Spence," Gran called back as they both moved to the top of the stairs.

Dressed in a faded red sweatshirt, jeans and his barn jacket, Spencer pounded up the stairs two at a time. He was carrying a black bag, much larger than the one he'd toted home from the office. His hair was mussed and his eyes were bright with excited concern. He flicked a glance at Alex, but zeroed in on his grandmother.

"Gran, I need you to watch the girls."

Gran was already reaching for a sweater hanging on a coat tree in the hall. "Got an emergency?"

"Yep. It's Dolly Ford. She's having the baby."

Gran stopped in her tracks. "I thought Josh delivered all their babies?"

Spence nodded tersely. "He has before—and done a good job of it, from what I've heard—but they were all normal deliveries. This one's turning out to be difficult.''

''Well why doesn't the blamed fool take her to the hospital?''

''He won't. You know he won't, Gran! He's a hardheaded jackass who fancies himself totally self-reliant in that log cabin retreat of theirs. The fact that he broke down and actually called *me* has me really worried. Oh, and I need your car.''

''What's wrong with *your* car?''

''I took it in two days ago to Waltons to have the brakes done, remember? I was going to pick it up tomorrow morning. Just haven't had time before, and now the shop's closed for the night. I could call Joe, but by the time he drove into town and opened up the shop—You get my drift.''

Irma propped her hands on her hips and scowled. ''But, Spence, I lent my car to Sylvia Westwood! She drove down to see her granddaughter in Ossipee for the weekend. Well, ain't this a heck of a situation! You're just going to have to call the paramedics, Spence.''

''The paramedics would never be able to—''

''Use my car, Spencer,'' Alex broke in. ''Better yet, I'll drive you there and help out if I can.''

Spencer scowled at her, but held out his hand for the keys. ''I appreciate your offer. I'll take the car, but you'd better stay put here at the house.''

''Either I go or you don't get the car.''

Spencer and Irma both gawked at her. ''Why on earth do you want to tag along?'' Irma wanted to know.

''Because I might be able to help,'' Alex insisted. ''I've witnessed and helped in a couple of births in primitive conditions that would make a log cabin retreat in New Hampshire look like the high-tech maternity ward at Cedar Sinai.''

''I don't have time to argue with you, Alex,'' Spencer barked, annoyed, obviously sure she'd be more in the way than an actual help. ''Let's go.''

While Irma headed for the house next door where the girls were already in bed and asleep, Spencer and Alex jogged down the streets they'd strolled up just a couple of hours earlier.

''Sorry to rush you,'' Spencer called over his shoulder. ''But I'm afraid this really might be an urgent situation.''

Alex didn't reply. The wind that had whipped up since nightfall would have just snatched her words away, anyway. She looked up at a sky overcast with fast-moving clouds. It looked like a storm was brewing. She was glad she had a jacket in the back seat of the car, because even running wasn't warming her up. She was glad, too, there was another camera stored with the jacket. She might take pictures, if the Fords allowed it.

In minutes they reached her car and she unlocked the driver's side door and scooted in, then reached for her jacket and slipped it on.

''Shouldn't I be driving?'' Spencer suggested. ''You don't know where they live.''

''Be my guest.'' She got out and ran around the back of the car to the other side, the two of them crossing paths like players in a Chinese fire drill.

''Nice car,'' Spencer commented as he sped away from the curb.

''My dad bought it for me.'' She wasn't sure why she'd told him that. Maybe she just wanted to convince him that her dad, whom he'd only seen pounding his fist and yelling before, was a nice guy. But since she couldn't tell him who her dad really was, what did she think she was accomplishing?

"Your dad must be very generous."

"He is. And since I won't allow him to be nearly as generous as he wants to be, it was a real kick for him to buy me this car."

"I'm just glad it's a four-wheel drive. Did I mention that the Fords' house is located halfway up a thickly wooded mountain and the only way to get there is over dirt roads with potholes you could hide an elephant in?"

"No, but if you think I'm worried about my new car, *don't* worry. I'm just glad my car and I are available to help out."

He looked over at her. The dim light that shone in from the street lamps outside revealed a quizzical expression. "You really do think you might be able to help me, don't you?"

Drolly she said, "Your faith in me is less than inspiring."

"How can I have faith in someone I don't even know?"

He was right. And, the bottom line was, he really shouldn't have faith in her. Not for any reason. Not in any situation. He didn't know her or who she really was. If he did, she'd be out on her fanny in less time than it took to say, "Stick out your tongue and say *ahh*."

"You'll just have to trust me on this one, Spencer," she assured him. "I really have assisted in a couple of births. I won't charge ahead on my own. If you happen to need some assistance—and that's an 'if'—just tell me what to do and I'll do it. I'm not squeamish. I won't faint or throw up.''

''You really are a gutsy gal, aren't you, Alex?'' he said. ''When I called to ask my grandmother if she'd put you up at the house and she recognized your name, she told me about all the places you've gone just to take pictures. I had no idea you were such an intrepid world traveler when I met you in the office.''

They were on the highway headed out of town now. By the light of the full moon that occasionally peeked out from behind the thickening clouds, Alex could see a mountain looming up in front of them. It certainly wasn't anything compared to the Rockies, the Himalayas or the Andes, but it was a fair-size bump of earth. Climbing it via a dirt road would be interesting. She just hoped it didn't start raining. Steep dirt roads that had turned into steep muddy roads could be hazardous.

''I'm beginning to think coming to New Hampshire was just as intrepid of me as going to China or Russia,'' she said dryly.

He grinned, his teeth catching the gleam of the moon. ''You could be right. But, remember, this was *your* idea.''

Chapter Six

This was my idea, Alex told herself over and over again as the Subaru climbed the slick, dark mountainside. Sure enough, fifteen minutes into the drive the clouds had mobilized into a solid storm front.

"I can't believe this," Alex murmured as the rain fell fast and furious, making it hard for the highly efficient windshield wipers on her brand-new, off-road vehicle to keep up with it. Then there was the mud that splashed up from the road...if you could call it a road. Heck, the ruts in it could hide a whole *herd* of elephants!

"I can believe it. My whole day has been like this. I just hope my rotten luck doesn't spill over onto my patient."

"Why do they live way up here?"

"When you meet Josh Ford, you'll understand."

"Is he—you know...?"

"Nuts? No. He just became disillusioned with civilization a few years ago and decided to raise his family away from it all. He means well, but sometimes his strict policy of self-reliance causes hardships for the people he loves the most. And he *does* love them."

"How many kids do they have?" Alex gripped the arm rest as the car slipped a few inches in the mud, coming disconcertingly close to the edge of the road...which dropped off a few hundred feet.

"Six." Spencer had righted the vehicle, answering her question without missing a beat.

Whew. She was certainly glad Spencer was driving and not her. He seemed to have nerves of steel.

"Six! That's a lot of kids."

"Yep. Boys, too."

"*All* of them?"

"Yep."

"I'll bet Dolly's hoping this one's a girl."

"I'll bet she doesn't allow herself to get her hopes up, anymore."

"How do they get to school? And don't tell me a bus climbs this mountain to pick them up."

"Dolly home-teaches them."

"Oh."

"Yeah, up here on the mountain and without even school to expose them to the real world, they're probably a little too sheltered. Don't get me wrong, I admire what the man is trying to do. I completely understand his desire to protect his children, but you can go too far."

She turned to look at him, but could see only the outline of his jaw in the dim light coming from the dashboard. It looked like he was clenching it.

"Having kids has changed you, hasn't it?" she said impulsively.

"In more ways than I ever imagined." He paused so long Alex thought he was finished, but then he added, "It was such a surprise, such a shock when

I found out Karlie wanted me to be their guardian. I've never liked surprises. Not since—''

''Not since Karlie left you at the altar for the girls' real father, right?'' Again she was being impulsive. Maybe even stupid.

Tersely he asked, ''How did you know about that?''

''Remember, I spent a good hour with Myra and longer than that with your grandmother. I pretty much know your whole history with the girls now.'' She was attributing too much of her knowledge to two innocent old ladies, but she needed to talk about these things and she needed scapegoats to explain how she'd received her information. She couldn't very well tell him she'd found out so many private details of his life from her father and her father's P.I.

''Well, you know too damn much then,'' he growled.

Alex supposed she should be offended by his tone of voice, but she wasn't surprised that he was ticked off, and she didn't blame him. In fact, she was suddenly covered in goose bumps from head to toe. She wasn't sure if it was because she was in peril of sliding off a mountainside to her death, the sexy timbre of his voice when he growled at her like that, or a combination of the two. But he obviously wasn't ready to spill his guts. She'd have to find out later if he had still been in love with Karlie when she died, one possible explanation for him to take on a lifetime of responsibility for her three little girls. But, Alex realized with a shock, it was not an explanation she especially cared for.

''We're almost there,'' he said a minute later, as the road widened and leveled off.

''What did Josh tell you about what's going on with Dolly? Does he know what's wrong?''

''He just said her water broke early this morning, she's fully dilated, but the baby won't drop into the birth canal. All her other labors have been short ones. This one's gone on for fourteen hours and she's weak as a kitten.''

''Do you think the baby's positioned wrong?''

''That seems most likely. I just hope this isn't a situation that can only be remedied by a cesarean.''

''Have yóu done one before?''

''Sure. Several. But only in hospitals.''

Suddenly a building loomed out of the rain. Sitting atop a grassy knoll, the two-story house was made out of logs, but Alex wouldn't call it a cabin, exactly. It was too big for that. From the light of lanterns hanging from the rafters of a porch that spanned the entire front length of the building, she had a good view of the place. It was pretty uneven in design, like a kid's rambling project made out of Lincoln Logs. Apparently Josh Ford did not have a natural bent toward architectural design, but it certainly looked sturdy.

The car skidded to a stop at the bottom of the knoll, Alex grabbed her purse and the spare camera, and they both stepped out into the downpour…and ankle-deep mud. ''That's what I get for wearing Gucci loafers,'' she shouted above the rain as she slipped around and the mud oozed into her shoes. ''I've got boots at home that are perfect for this. Too bad I'm not wearing them.''

''This was your idea,'' he reminded her, coming

around to her side of the car. "I could have come alone. Hell, I should have put my foot down and *insisted* that I come alone! I've exposed you to danger."

"Nix the guilt thing, Spencer. I wouldn't have given you the keys if you'd put your foot down. Quaint phrase...*put your foot down,* isn't it? I wonder what it means? Put your foot down exactly *where?*"

"We're getting wet. Here, hold on to me. Those soles are useless in this stuff."

Transferring the black bag to his left hand, Spencer threw his right arm around Alex's waist. Without his support, Alex wasn't sure she'd have been able to climb out of the mud and up the hill without falling on her rear. But it wasn't just gratitude that was making her heart flutter. It was his close proximity and the masterful way he was handling the situation. What a guy! Too bad he had to be on the other side of the war she was waging, and he'd eventually find out she was a spy for the enemy.

"Dr. Jones! It's you! You're finally here!"

A tall, thin boy Alex guessed roughly to be ten or eleven, dressed in jeans and a hooded sweatshirt, stood on the porch and flapped his arms excitedly.

"How's your mother, Jacob?"

Now on the porch, Spencer removed his arm from around Alex's waist and ran splayed fingers through his damp hair. Alex ran a hand through her own short hair, too, and felt the droplets of water running down her face and neck. They both removed their muddy shoes to leave on the porch.

"I don't know," was Jacob's anxious reply. "Dad shut the door to their bedroom and sent me out here to watch for you. Mom's making a lot of noise…and that's not like Mom. Hurry!''

Jacob held the door open and stood to the side. As she and Spencer passed through the entrance and into the softly lighted interior, Alex felt Jacob's curious gaze.

The house was open and high-ceilinged, much more pleasant inside than Alex had anticipated. It was clean and warm, the front room heated by a large fireplace, and there was an aura of domestic comfort that paid tribute to the Fords' ability to make a home out of an uneven, oversize cabin. A woman's touch was apparent everywhere, from the homemade cushions on the big, worn sofa, to the doilies on the simple wooden tables. Alex was also relieved to note that they had electricity, undoubtedly supplied by a generator. But where were the other five boys hiding?

Spencer and Alex pulled off their jackets and laid them on a chair. Alex left her purse, but took her camera. ''Which way—''

Spencer's question was answered when they heard a keening moan coming from a hallway on the opposite side of the room. Alex followed as Spencer hurried toward the hallway and the closed door at the end of it, but as she passed the stairs, she looked up and saw five pair of eyes staring down at them. Jacob's brothers were keeping vigil from the rustic banisters above. The youngest looked no more than two years old.

She tried to give them a reassuring smile, but their only response was the same curious and startled gaze she'd received from Jacob. She supposed that having Dr. Jones there at all was enough of a novelty without her—a total stranger in town—showing up with him.

She followed Spencer into the room and closed the door behind her. It was a small room almost completely filled with a queen-size bed with tall newel posts rising from the oak headboard and footboard. She'd thought the boys looked surprised to see her, but it was nothing compared to the look she got from their father.

Josh Ford was a tall, spare man with a head of thick dark hair and a handsome face. In his bib overalls, he reminded her of Henry Fonda in *The Grapes of Wrath,* only older. When they came in, he was bending over his small, blond wife. Dolly Ford's delicate features were pinched with pain, her eyes closed. As Josh stood up and turned his head, the anxiety he was feeling on her behalf clearly showed in his eyes. His anguished gaze fell first on Spencer, resulting in a flicker of relief, but when he saw Alex, he seemed to close up like a threatened oyster.

"Who's she and what's she doing here?"

"Her name is Alex, and she's here to help me, Josh," Spencer clipped out as he set down his medical bag on a table by the bed, opened it and began to pull out instruments and supplies. Judging by the paraphernalia that already littered the table, including two bowls—the big one undoubtedly for the placenta, the smaller one probably there in case Dolly got sick—sterile gauze pads, a stethoscope, antiseptic hand soap and a glass of juice with a flexible straw, etc., Alex figured Josh really did know what he was doing. But that was only if it was a straightforward, normal delivery.

"Is she a midwife or a nurse?"

"No, she's a photographer."

"A photographer!"

He eyed her camera, which she immediately set aside on a nearby table.

"She's helped deliver babies before."

"Hell, so have I. That doesn't mean—"

"Don't cuss, Josh," came a soft, breathless voice from the bed. "And don't be so unfriendly."

Alex looked over Spencer's bent shoulder and saw Dolly's eyes open. She looked exhausted, but she focused on Alex and gave her a tremulous smile. "It's good to have another woman around for a change...especially at a time like this."

Alex smiled back. "Thank you, Mrs. Ford."

"Call me Dolly," she said before her eyes closed and her mouth twisted with another contraction.

"Don't be stoic because you have company, Dolly," Alex advised her, moving around to the other side of the bed and laying her hand on the woman's shoulder.

Dolly nodded, a tear squeezing out from under a closed lid, but she still didn't make a sound.

"What took you so long, Jones?" Josh demanded, moving on to another point of irritation since being asked by his wife to leave Alex alone.

By now Spencer had arranged his medical tools and snapped on his rubber gloves. He ignored Josh, none-too-subtly crowded him away from the bed and bent over Dolly. "Sorry I didn't say hello before, Dolly, but your husband has bombarded me with questions from the get-go."

She opened her eyes and managed another smile. "I know, Dr. Jones. You'll have to excuse him, though. He's just worried about me."

"Don't make excuses for *me*," Josh muttered.

"I'll excuse him," Spencer assured her with a pat on the arm. "He wouldn't have called me if he wasn't really worried about you. What's going on?"

"I told you. She's sick and weak and the baby won't drop," Josh explained impatiently. "I think he's turned wrong. I don't think it's breech. Maybe posterior, though. She's had a lot of back pain."

"My contractions are coming one right on top of the other, Dr. Jones. Josh says I'm fully dilated. Why won't the baby come?"

"I'm going to examine you and see if I can figure that out, Dolly. Are you ready?"

"I was ready a few hours ago," she murmured, then clenched her jaw as another pain claimed her.

Unless asked to do something else, Alex decided that the best way to help out would be to soothe, comfort and help Dolly to relax. She grabbed a damp washcloth that was resting on the pillow by Dolly's tangled hair, dipped it in a nearby basin of cool water and wiped the beads of sweat off her brow and upper lip.

"Contrary to what the poetically inclined like to say about this whole process, childbirth doesn't exactly make a woman beautiful, does it?" Dolly joked weakly.

"Forgive me for sounding poetic myself, Dolly, but you'll be glowing like a rose once the baby comes," Alex assured her. "New mothers are always beautiful."

Spencer began the exam while Josh looked on, asked questions and made comments. To distract Dolly, Alex kept up a steady flow of low-voiced conversation, stretching out the answer to Dolly's question about her work as a photographer, talking about herself and the places she'd traveled to, since Dolly obviously wasn't up to answering questions about herself.

"I want to push!" Dolly cried out after an especially hard contraction that made her whimper.

"Not yet, Dolly. Hold on just a few minutes longer." Spencer stood up and came to the head of the bed. "The baby isn't breech."

"Thank God!"

"But Josh was right. He's in a posterior position. He's ready to be born, but he can't get past the curve of your pelvis without a little help."

"You don't mean—?"

"No, I don't think you'll need a cesarean. The baby's heart rate is a little erratic, though, so we need to hurry, but I think I can turn him around with forceps."

She sighed shakily. "Do whatever you need to do, Doc."

Spencer turned to Josh, who nodded soberly.

For this last stage of the delivery, Josh took Alex's place by his wife, soothed her, bathed her face and held her hand, while Spencer worked to get the baby into the right position for a successful birth. Alex helped whenever she could.

It was a very tense few minutes, but so exhilarating when Spencer finally gave Dolly the go-ahead to push and the baby's head crowned, then slipped out easily, faceup, just the way he was supposed to! His head was a little misshapen from the forceps, but Alex knew that that was only temporary and thought he—make that *she*—was the most beautiful baby in the world.

Spencer's face lit up and he shared a big smile with Alex before making the announcement, "It's a girl!"

"Well, I'll be damned," Josh choked out, staring down at the messy little bundle Spencer was cupping in his big hands. She was crying, her tiny fists and legs held in the air and quivering like tender blades of new grass in a spring breeze.

"Can I take a picture?" Alex asked.

Josh nodded absently and Alex clicked away.

"Take her, Josh," Spencer ordered, still grinning like a lottery winner. "Hold your daughter for a minute, then hand her over to your wife. She certainly deserves this little girl. She worked hard enough for her."

Josh took the baby gingerly, his eyes welling with tears. "I've never held my own baby girl before."

Spencer chuckled. "They're no more fragile than baby boys."

Josh stared down at his daughter for maybe thirty seconds, then handed her to Dolly, who'd been silently smiling and weeping ever since Spencer's announcement.

"I can't believe it!" she whispered brokenly as she held her newborn baby in her trembling arms. "A little girl at last! Spencer Jones, you must be a good-luck charm!"

When Spencer didn't come back with a joking remark, Alex looked up at him as they both stood over the happy couple and this latest, most welcome addition to their family. His eyes were shiny with moisture, the expression one of awe...and envy?

"You're lucky, Josh," Spencer said at last. "Not every man gets to witness the birth of his children."

Josh beamed. "Hell, I know how lucky I am. Isn't she a beauty? Just like her mother."

"She'll look even prettier once she's cleaned up," Dolly murmured as she stroked the baby's face with a finger.

"You know what to do, Josh," Spencer said. "You've done it before enough times. I've still got work to do."

"Alex?"

Alex was startled when Josh directly addressed her. "Yes?" she asked anxiously, expecting him to order her out of the room so they could privately enjoy this blessed occasion.

But Josh looked chagrined. "I'm too shaky to clean up the baby. I might drop her, and that'd be a damned shame after waiting so long for her, now wouldn't it? Would...would *you* clean her up?"

Alex flushed with pleasure. She caught Spencer's eye and he smiled approvingly. "I'd love to do the honors, Josh."

And it *was* an honor...almost a sacred ritual, really, to bathe and wrap the baby in a blanket, then place her again in her mother's waiting arms. While so pleasantly occupied, Alex even thought she heard ticking... The ticking of her own biological clock!

"I want to call her Amelia, Josh. Amy for short," Dolly said. "After your mother."

Josh beamed some more.

Later, after Dolly was cleaned up and made comfortable, the room put to order, and the baby fed its first meal at her mother's breast, Josh brought the boys in. They stood around the bed, wide-eyed and shy, staring at the tiny, red-faced scrap of humanity that was their little sister.

"Well, that little girl won't have to worry about being picked on or taken advantage of," Spencer whispered to Alex as he packed up the last of his instruments into the medical bag. "She's got half a dozen built-in bodyguards. I'd hate to be the fella that comes courtin' up this mountain."

Before Alex could think about what she was saying, she retorted teasingly, "Look who's talking. I bet you'll be one of those fathers that interrogates his daughters' dates so thoroughly, all the boys will be terrified to ask the girls out a second time."

Spencer grinned. "You're probably right."

But then Alex realized that if she had her way about things, Spencer wouldn't be the one interrogating the girls' future dates! That pleasure and duty would belong to her father...the girls' real grandfather, Richard Ethington the Second. For the first time, a doubt about whether or not her father really was the best choice to serve as the girls' guardian entered her mind.

Horrified and feeling disloyal, Alex thrust the doubt aside. Of course her father was the best choice! Just because Spencer was a nice guy and was obviously attached to the girls didn't mean he ought to be their guardian. He'd only had the girls for two and a half months, hardly long enough to make it disastrously traumatic to take them away from their present home situation and place them in another, *better* home situation.

Sure, Camilla seemed to adore Spencer—and vice versa—but she was just a baby. She'd forget him and adjust quickly to a new daddy. And as for Elizabeth and Margaret, they might miss Gran, but they'd probably be quite happy to say goodbye to

"Dr. Jones," a man who, after nearly three months, they still didn't speak to.

"I don't think you should try to drive down the mountain tonight," Josh was saying as he followed Spencer and Alex out of the bedroom, shutting the door quietly behind him. "I think you should stay here till morning."

"Stay here?" Alex caught herself repeating stupidly. "Er...all night?"

"I know what you're thinking," Josh continued with a faint smile.

She seriously doubted it.

"You're wondering where you'd sleep, right? Well, you're correct in assuming that space is at a premium around here, but I've got sleeping bags you could spread out in front of the fire in the living room. You'd be snug as bugs."

Alex darted an alarmed glance at Spencer, whose calm demeanor seemed to indicate that he wasn't nearly as perturbed as she was by the idea of the two of them sleeping side by side in front of a cozy fire. Maybe she'd overestimated the extent of his attraction to her, but, if anything, she'd *under*estimated her attraction to him. Her whole body was suddenly warm and tingling at the mere thought of lying down next to this man, touching or not.

She stared at him, at the deep-blue eyes that had misted with emotions moments before, but which now had taken on a smoky and seductive hue in the dim lighting.

Her fascinated gaze took in the sexy, tousled hair, still a little damp at the edges.

Then the lips. Mmm, very kissable looking.

And the broad shoulders. Strong, powerful. Begging to be caressed.

Last and best of all, she stared at the big, beautifully shaped hands that had so capably guided little Amelia into the world, then held her aloft for everyone to see and marvel over.

Those hands looked just as capable of guiding a woman to a delirious state of ecstasy....

"What's the matter, Alex?" Spencer asked, his eyes narrowed and questioning.

"Nothing," she lied, looking down at her stocking feet. She was aghast at the way her mind had fashioned a sexual fantasy from start to finish, starring herself and the unsuspecting Dr. Spencer Jones, simply because she might share a floor with him! She hoped, among his many talents, he wasn't able to read minds! "I thought I heard it quit raining a half hour ago."

Josh nodded. "It did, but it rained hard enough that the road's going to stay muddy and slick for a couple of days or longer. And the clouds are still thick, blocking out most of the moonlight." He glanced back and forth from Alex to Spencer, then shrugged. "But if you're dead-set on leaving, I'll drive you down. I know the turns and dips in the road well enough to get you safely to the bottom of the mountain, after which you'd be perfectly fine, but—"

"No, Josh," Spencer said flatly. "You're nearly as exhausted as Dolly. I wouldn't dream of allowing you to drive us down the mountain. And since I haven't got any pressing appointments to keep first thing in the morning, I see no reason why we shouldn't play it safe and camp in front of your fire tonight." Spencer turned to Alex again. The expression in his eyes was frustratingly unreadable. "How about you, Alex? You got any pressing appointments in the morning?"

She stared at him, thinking about the phrase "play it safe" he'd just used as an argument for staying the night in the Ford cabin. In Alex's opinion, it would be safer to risk their necks driving down the mountain than risk their emotions sharing sleeping quarters…even if they did have separate sleeping bags.

"Well, I'm still not convinced we need to stay over. We made it up here, didn't we?"

"By the skin of our teeth," Spencer reminded her dryly.

"But I really need to get out early tomorrow and take some shots of the trees in the morning light while they're still wet from the storm."

"We'll leave at first light," he assured her.

"And don't worry about not waking up in time," Josh added before she could voice additional concerns. "Red, our rooster, will wake you up at the crack of dawn. We're used to him, but I'm sure he'll wake you two city slickers up with no trouble at all."

"What about the girls?" Alex asked as a last desperate argument.

"The girls are fine with Gran. I'll call her right now and tell her what's going on and that we'll see her first thing in the morning. If we leave early enough, the girls won't know I was even gone."

Alex could think of nothing else to say, painfully aware her reluctance must seem very odd and unreasonable. But she couldn't help it. She'd decided to keep Spencer Jones at arm's length, knew it was the wisest course of action for them both, and now she was faced with hours of temptation to behave any way *but* wisely. Not that she could actually fool around in a houseful of children, but the torture of *wanting* to would be bad enough!

"Listen, Alex, I'm sorry if this interferes with your plans, but it was your idea to accompany me, if you remember. I have no intention of risking an accident, not with those three little girls depending on me," Spencer said in a tone of finality that clearly indicated that, as far as he was concerned, the matter was settled. "They've already lost one set of parents."

Well, if something happened to you, they'd be sent to where they really belong...with their grandfather! was Alex's first frustrated thought.

She was immediately sorry she'd even thought such a thing. She did not wish for anything bad to happen to Spencer Jones. In fact, her mind was becoming increasingly occupied with imagining *good* things she'd like to have happen to Spencer Jones. Good things *she'd* make happen...say, in front of a cozy fire? Damn it, who'd have thought she'd needed to bring a lasso to Jonesville for roping in her rogue libido!

"So, it's settled? You're staying?" Josh asked. He looked at Alex, one brow cocked at an inquiring angle. Was she imagining it, or did Josh look amused by this whole thing? She *must* be imagining it. What was there to be amused about? She wasn't amused.

"It's settled," she agreed with a nonchalant shrug of her shoulders. "We'll stay. It's no big deal."

"Could have fooled me," Spencer murmured as he pulled an extremely compact cell phone from a back pocket of his jeans.

Alex ignored the comment. "If we're up and out of here at dawn, I'll still be able to get the pictures I want."

"Good," Josh said with satisfaction. "That's a load off my mind. I'll send the boys off to bed now and get you those sleeping bags while I'm upstairs tucking in the little ones." He turned to go, then turned back with a frown. "Oh, by the way, Doc." He shot a quick, embarrassed glance at Alex and lowered his voice to a gruff whisper. "Dolly'll be in to see you as soon as she's up to it. We're in agreement, especially after what she went through today, that this baby'll be our last. She'll be needing some…you know…" His voice lowered even further. "Birth control pills or something."

Spencer nodded understandingly. "No problem, Josh. Have her call Velma for an appointment. We'll fit her in whenever it's convenient for Dolly."

Josh smiled and nodded, satisfied. "Thanks, Doc. Thanks for everything." They shook hands, both men smiling with genuine warmth at each other.

As Josh went back into the bedroom and Spencer made his phone call, Alex wandered into the living room and stared at the oval-shaped braided rug in front of the fireplace, her arms folded over her chest, her bottom lip caught between her teeth.

Spencer soon followed and stood next to her, staring at the same spot. "Looks cozy enough to me, Alex," he said.

Too cozy, Alex thought miserably.

He leaned close. Close enough that she could

smell the faint tang of his aftershave and the warm male scent that belonged to him alone. "In all your travels, from time to time I'm sure you've had to throw down your sleeping bag next to a man's. Other journalists, other photographers. How's this time any different? What's bugging you, Alex?"

"*You're* what's bugging me," Alex blurted.

Chapter Seven

Spencer raised a brow. "*I'm* what's bugging you? Would you like to explain, Alex?"

"Well, I..." Alex spluttered. No, she wouldn't like to explain. In fact she'd like to kick herself for blurting out those frustrated words in the first place.

He walked around to stand in front of her—very close—his arms crossed over his broad chest, stretching the fabric of his faded sweatshirt over what were obviously very nice pecs. Did the good doctor have time to work out in the gym, or was he just naturally buff? He gazed down at her, his eyes searching hers. His voice was low-pitched and sexily insinuating. "Or would you rather *I* explained it?"

"You...you think you can?" she asked in a small voice.

"Yes, I think I can. And I think it's about time we were honest with each other."

No, not that! Not honesty, Alex thought, in a panic. While she believed in honesty as much as the next guy, she'd been forced to make an exception in this case. She couldn't be honest with Spencer and accomplish the important thing she'd come there to do. But being dishonest with someone as up-front and genuine as Spencer Jones was becoming more and more difficult.

"Dolly made some oatmeal cookies last night," Josh said, stopping by before going upstairs. "Feel like a midnight snack?"

"Thanks, but I'm not—" Spencer began.

"Oatmeal cookies! My favorite," Alex exclaimed. "Lead the way!"

"Jacob will help you to the cookies and some cocoa while I get your sleeping bags and settle the little boys into bed," Josh said as he led them into the kitchen and left them in the care of his oldest son. "See you in a few minutes."

Alex was grateful for the reprieve and took full advantage of it. She bombarded Jacob with friendly questions and prevented the shy but polite boy from leaving even after he had supplied them with big mugs of hot instant cocoa and placed a plate of cookies on the table in front of them. The poor kid was obviously itching to escape.

Spencer did not join in the conversation, but merely sipped his cocoa, listened and watched with a sardonic expression that indicated he knew exactly what Alex was doing...avoiding a private conversation with him. She knew she was only putting off the inevitable, but she was playing this scene moment by desperate moment.

Alex had run out of questions and Jacob was backing toward the door when Josh showed up again. When he saw his father, Jacob bolted out of the room and could be heard pounding up the stairs as if he were being chased by ghosts.

Josh scratched his head. "Never seen the boy so eager to go to bed."

"I think he was trying to get away from Alex," Spencer told him with a twinkle in his eyes. "She's asked him everything from his shoe size to his favorite Spice Girl."

Josh's eyes narrowed. "What's a Spice Girl?"

Spencer chuckled. "Jacob didn't know, either. No MTV around here, I gather."

"No TV, period," Josh said with satisfaction.

"I was just trying to be friendly," Alex insisted defensively, but she and Spencer both knew that was a lie. Jacob seemed like a nice kid she'd enjoy getting to know under normal circumstances, but tonight she'd blatantly used him to avoid a tête-à-tête with Spencer.

Josh looked keenly back and forth between the two of them, but let the subject drop. "I've got your sleeping bags laid out in the living room. Don't think you'll need extra blankets, but there's some in the hall closet if you do. There's extra toothbrushes in the bathroom, still in their packaging, in the bottom drawer of the vanity. Probably won't see you in the morning before you leave, so take care getting down the mountain, okay? If you want some breakfast before you go, there's homemade bread for toast and some milk in the fridge. Dolly makes a delicious omelet, but I don't think she'll be up to—"

"Of course not, Josh. We'll be fine," Spencer assured him. "Gran makes pancakes every Saturday morning. I think we can hold off eating till then. Don't you, Alex?"

She was pretty sure she could hold off eating and even *breathing* till then. She certainly wasn't going to be able to relax as long as she was sharing such close quarters with Spencer. "We'll be fine," Alex repeated with a forced smile for their concerned host. "Go be with your wife and new baby and don't give us another thought. It was nice meeting you, Josh."

He looked and sounded surprised as he answered, "It was nice meeting you, too, Alex." He slid a quick glance at Spencer. "And—who knows?— maybe we'll see you around."

Not unless he was planning on being in town that weekend, thought Alex. After that she'd be gone, and soon after that Spencer would know who she really was and she'd be about as welcome in Jonesville as the bubonic plague.

When neither Spencer nor Alex spoke, Josh said in parting, "Well, good night, folks. Sleep tight."

Alone at last, Spencer thought. He liked Josh, but he required privacy for what he was about to do. Alexandra's revealing behavior since finding out they were going to be sleeping on the floor together had convinced him once and for all that she was, indeed, as turned on by him as he was by her and having an honest conversation to defuse the situation was the smartest thing to do. Surely two mature, intelligent adults could acknowledge a problem, talk about it and solve it.

And it *was* a problem. They simply couldn't get involved. She had a fiancé and he had a girlfriend who was eminently suitable to become a mother to his three little girls. Oh…and she'd be a good wife for him, too, of course.

"You've still got a full mug of cocoa there," he commented as Alexandra avoided his eyes and stirred the chocolate mixture. "And you haven't touched the cookies. I thought oatmeal were your favorite?''

"They are," Alexandra insisted guiltily. She grabbed a cookie and gave him a belligerent look. "I plan to eat at least a half dozen of these and finish my cocoa, so you'd better go on to bed. I'm sure you're tired and there's no reason to wait for me."

"Oh, but there's a *very* good reason to wait for you, Alex," Spencer assured her. "We started a conversation about honesty and you're not going to weasel out of it. Bring your cocoa and cookies with you and we'll talk by the fire. It's getting a little cold in here."

Alexandra's lovely lips compressed into a stubborn line. "I'm not cold."

He glanced at the smooth olive skin inside the V of her sweater and at her wrists below her sweater sleeves. "Then why do you have goose bumps?" He'd noticed that her nipples had hardened, too, but he didn't dare mention those. He'd be better off not noticing them again, either, considering how his body was responding.

"I have no idea what this 'honesty' conversation is supposed to be about," Alexandra complained, "or why you're commenting on my goose bumps."

"If you won't go in by the fire where it's warm, we'll talk here." He took a deep breath, then leveled with her. "Alex, we might as well admit that we're attracted to each other and deal with it."

Her alarmed and guilty look said it all. "What makes you think I'm attracted to you? *Men!* You're all egotists! If you don't mind, I'm going to brush my teeth and go to bed." With her nose in the air, she dropped the cookie on the plate, got up and proceeded to stomp out of the kitchen.

Spencer stood up and caught her wrist as she was leaving, then swung her around gently to face him. Her expression as she looked up at him was startled, her gray-green eyes wide and questioning, her full lips parted on a gasp. He had only intended to block her huffy departure from the kitchen, but with her standing so close, looking so good and smelling so sweet...

For the second time in one day, Spencer pulled a surprised female into his arms and kissed her.

But the second time was much different from the first.

This time he felt something.

And it wasn't resistance on her part. If he for one second sensed that Alexandra wanted him to stop, he'd stop. But after an initial stiffness in her lips and posture, she seemed to literally melt against him. She wrapped her arms around his neck and leaned into the kiss, her lips becoming soft and pliant. The kiss evolved from tentative, to curious, to fiery in a matter of seconds. Her fingers found their way into his hair. His hands roamed her back and shoulders, then settled on either side of her slim hips, holding them flush against his.

When they finally came up for air, they stared into each other's eyes, both dazed, both amazed at how quickly their desire for each other had ignited, then escalated. It seemed like a perfect moment for Spencer to make his point.

"I believe you've just proved me right, Alex," he said in a husky whisper. "If this isn't mutual attraction, what is it?"

She blinked, focused, then blushed. Biting her bottom lip, she untwined her arms from around his neck and quickly left the kitchen. Spencer took a deep breath and blew it out. He couldn't believe what had just happened! He'd only wanted to talk to her, to "defuse" the situation by getting things out in the open and dealing with them. Instead he'd only made things worse by kissing her.

They still needed to talk. They needed to list, out loud, all the reasons they could never kiss again.

Spencer gave his emotions and body a moment to recover, then picked up his mug and the plate of cookies, flipped off the kitchen light with his elbow and followed Alexandra into the living room.

Not surprisingly, he found her dragging her sleeping bag to the other end of the room, far away from the light and warmth of the fireplace. Far away from *him*.

"I have no intention of ravaging you," he said ruefully.

"Did you intend to kiss me?"

"Well, no. That just kind of happened."

"I rest my case, Dr. Jones," she muttered as she bent over to arrange and plump her pillow. He couldn't help but notice again what a nicely shaped rear chassis she had. *Damn.*

He set the plate of cookies on a low table next to the fireplace and sat down on top of the other sleeping bag, crossing his legs pretzel-style. The fire was just right, not too hot, and it cast a circle of golden light on the immediate surroundings. The room was cozy. *Too cozy.*

He forged on, trying to sound casual. "So, it's back to Dr. Jones, eh?"

"I think that's best," she said stiffly.

"I think we still need to talk. There've been sparks flying between us ever since you showed up at my office today." Spencer deliberately spoke louder than necessary.

She straightened up and turned quickly. "*Shh!* You'll wake up the whole household!"

He raised the volume another notch. "With you clear over there, you won't be able to hear me unless I speak up."

She flapped her hands at him to quiet down. "Okay! Okay! You win." She pulled the sleeping bag back in front of the fireplace, plopped down and crossed her arms as well as her legs. She glared at him, looking about as approachable as a porcupine with its quills at full alert. "I'm here, but I'm not happy about it. I see no reason to talk about a few errant sparks."

He chuckled softly, hoping she didn't notice the nervous edge to his laughter. He was having a hard time not reaching out and grabbing her. "I don't know why you're resisting this conversation. It's going to make us both feel much more comfortable once it's over."

"We kissed. No big deal. What's there to talk about?"

Piqued, he retorted, "It may have been 'no big deal' to you, but we can never let it happen again. We're both spoken for. You even more than me. You're engaged to be married, Alex."

"Hey, you kissed me, not the other way around!" she snapped defensively.

"But you kissed me back. Quite convincingly, I

might add. And you flirted with me at the office. You flirted *first*.''

She gave a strangled laugh. ''Must you be so—''

''Honest? That's what we need to be right now. Honest.''

''No, I was going to say 'immature.' And I'm just as bad…arguing over who did what first! We both sound like a couple of junior high students!''

She was right. His laugh was genuine this time and she joined him. They ended up grinning sheepishly at each other.

''I'm sorry,'' he said. ''I'm actually striving to be mature by having this conversation. It's always helped to talk things out with my patients—''

''But I'm not your patient,'' she reminded him.

''You were to begin with. And that's when all this started. Admit it, the chemistry between us is why you didn't want to stay here tonight, isn't it? Because you thought we might be tempted, at least in some small degree, to give in to our mutual attraction.''

''In a house this full of children, I could resist even Brad Pitt,'' Alex retorted. ''And that's while sharing the same sleeping bag. I can resist you, too, Spencer Jones.''

''Alex…you didn't exactly resist me in the kitchen.''

She grimaced, like a kid cornered and coerced into telling the truth. ''Okay, I admit it! I'm attracted to you! But you knew that already, didn't you? Why did you make me say it?''

Yes, he did know it already, but her spoken admission sent a thrill down his spine he hadn't expected. His plan to handle the situation by getting things out in the open seemed to be backfiring!

"And, yes, I was a little nervous about camping out with you like this," she continued in the beleaguered tone of one making a reluctant confession. "But not because I thought we couldn't control ourselves."

Spencer nodded doubtfully.

"I was more concerned about the way it might look to your...you know...girlfriend."

"I see," he said gravely. "Well, that's certainly considerate of you. Did you also worry about how it might seem to your *fiancé* if he found out?"

"Dimitri will never find out. Besides, Dimitri understands and trusts me. In my work, I camp out with men all the time."

"But it's different with me because—"

Impatiently she agreed, "Yes, I know it's different. But I'm certainly not going to explain *that* to Dimitri!"

"But wouldn't Dimitri—"

"Dimitri, Dimitri, Dimitri! Sheesh. I'm almost wishing I hadn't told you about him."

"But you did tell me about him, and now I want to know why his mere existence wasn't reason enough not to flirt with me. I know if *I* were Dimitri—"

"You're not. And you don't understand our relationship."

He shook his head, his brow furrowed. "I sure don't."

She launched a counterattack. "I don't understand your relationship with Bernice, either. Knowing your attraction to me, why weren't you as nervous as I was about staying here tonight?''

Hell, who said he wasn't nervous? But better she didn't know how much. He rested his mug on his knee, his thumb hooked in the handle. Summoning his most confident tone of voice, the one he used when reassuring frightened patients, he explained, ''Oh, I've got all kinds of compelling reasons—in addition to Bernice—for not being worried about you and me sleeping together.''

She raised her brows. ''*Sleeping* together?'

''Er...unfortunate terminology. Sorry. I meant 'camping' together.''

''That's better. So tell me the compelling reasons. That's what you want to do, isn't it?''

It wasn't what he wanted to do, it was what he needed to do. But, although he knew he had compelling reasons to avoid an involvement with Alexandra Koskov, in that moment, while looking at her in the firelight, he couldn't seem to remember them.

Her hair had gotten curlier from their dousing in the rain and she looked adorable. Not like a puppy was adorable, mind you. No sir. Not like a puppy at all.

His gaze lowered and lingered on those gorgeous lips of hers. An overwhelming compulsion to kiss her was stealing over him as it had in the kitchen. He couldn't remember his compelling reasons, but he had no problem recalling in precise and delicious detail how soft her lips had felt, how good her mouth had tasted.

Snap out of it, Jones! he told himself, determinedly wrenching his gaze away from those kiss-able lips.

"I've got responsibilities now," he said firmly. "I've got three little girls and a future to plan, *with* them and *for* them. Bernice would fit easily into that future. You, on the other hand—"

"Yes. Go on," she prompted him, her head tilted to the side, her eyes fixed intently on his face. Gone for the moment was her defensive mode. She seemed genuinely interested in where he thought she "fit."

He took a deep breath. "You, Alexandra Koskov, are engaged to a rich dude named Dimitri, have a glamorous career that takes you to the far corners of the earth and are just passing through this little burg. All that we could hope to gain from giving in to our attraction to each other is…is—" he swallowed against a throat that suddenly felt as dry and scratchy as tumbleweed "—a few days of steamy, romance-novel passion."

Following this little speech, neither of them spoke again for several minutes, as if they were sharing a mutual wistfulness for what could never be. As if just "a few days of steamy, romance-novel passion" sounded as good to her, as tempting, as it did to him.

Finally she broke the charged silence by wryly observing, "I thought you said this conversation was supposed to make us feel more comfortable."

He chuckled. "I thought it would. I *hoped* it would."

"I was afraid it wouldn't and I was right. Some-times honesty is just a plain bad idea, Spencer Jones, and you can quote me on that."

"Well, it cleared the air, didn't it?"

More like supercharged it with enough tension to wind up Big Ben, Alex thought. Spencer's plan hadn't worked. Admitting to an attraction didn't make it go away. It just confirmed that he was battling the same temptations she was. Wasn't the kiss proof enough of that without having to spill their guts to each other? Honesty had only made them more vulnerable. She knew it and he knew it, too.

But despite a growing desire to have a passionate fling with Spencer Jones, Alex was more determined than ever to keep him at arm's length. After all, Spencer honored honesty, and the only thing she'd truthfully 'fessed up to was her attraction to him. In every other way, in the ways that mattered most to him, she was being dangerously dishonest.

Spencer Jones deserved better than to get tangled up with a modern-day female version of Benedict Arnold.

"I think we'd better get some rest, don't you?" Alex suggested soberly.

Spencer smiled and nodded, looking defeated, apologetic and far too sexy with his rumpled hair and in his faded jeans and sweatshirt. "Yeah. Tomorrow's going to be a busy day."

Alex tore her gaze away from the arresting spectacle of Spencer by firelight and stood up. "Mind if I use the bathroom first?"

"Be my guest."

En route to the bathroom, Alex thought about how much had happened that day. That morning she and Spencer had been strangers, and tonight they were in the intimate situation of sharing a bathroom…not to mention sleeping with a mere two feet of floor between them. One little accidental roll and they could wake up nose to nose.

Alex forced that thought away as she brushed her teeth with one of the new toothbrushes from the vanity drawer and washed off the makeup she'd put on that morning just for Spencer Jones. Gazing at her reflection in the mirror, at her fresh-scrubbed cheeks and humidity-induced curls, she thought of Spencer and watched her cheeks grow even pinker.

When she returned to the living room, Spencer immediately got up and took his turn in the bathroom. While he was gone, she quickly slipped into the sleeping bag, fully clothed, and turned on her side, facing the wall. She squirmed around a little, knowing she'd be more comfortable if she took off her slacks, but she didn't dare. What if she had no privacy in the morning to put them back on?

When she heard him returning to the room, she squeezed her eyes shut and pretended to be asleep. She listened, her nerves as taut as a high-wire, at the unmistakable sound of a man removing his jeans. Then she heard him slip between the downy layers of the sleeping bag and imagined him, stretched full length inside...all sexy, sinewy, warm male. She remembered their kiss, every delicious moment in his arms, and how it felt being pressed against him, hip to hip.

"'Night, Alex," came his deep, drowsy voice out of the darkness, making the back of her neck tingle and her heart race. "Rest well."

Rest well. Yeah, right.

ALEX WAS UP THE NEXT morning even before Red the Rooster had had a chance to crow his usual wake-up call. It was still dark outside, but her glow-in-the-dark wristwatch said five-thirty and she was all for getting out of there as soon as possible.

She had probably slept that night a total of three hours—those three hours not continuous but broken into a few minutes here and there between tossing and turning and wrestling with her conscience. The wee, dark, wakeful hours of the night had forced her to admit that she not only lusted for Spencer Jones, but she also respected and admired him, too.

She was having doubts. She was beginning to think she should never have come there under false pretenses no matter how noble her motivation. She was beginning to wish there was some other way to help her father without having to hurt and betray a man like Spencer Jones.

And what *was* the best thing for those girls? Where did they belong? She was no longer sure.

She peered over at Spencer's sleeping bag and, since the fire was completely out, could barely make out the dark silhouette of his reposing body. He lay still as a stone. During the night, she hadn't noticed him tossing and turning like she had. Darn him. The very least he could have done was lose sleep, too! He didn't snore, either, just making him a little more perfect. Darn him again.

She crept out of her sleeping bag and tiptoed carefully across the cold floor, around the black, looming shapes of furniture, to the bathroom, grabbing her purse on the way. Spencer had told her sometime the previous evening that the house had a furnace that was fueled by propane, same as their water heater, but Josh didn't turn it on till after Thanksgiving. In the meantime, the family kept warm with layers of clothing and heat from the several fireplaces and potbellied stoves in the house. But no one was up to make fires and Alex shivered while she freshened up and brushed her chattering teeth.

Combing through her hair, she guessed the air was still full of humidity because the curls stayed. She dabbed on a bit of mascara and some lipstick and made a face at herself for doing so. If she really wanted to discourage Spencer's attraction to her, wouldn't she just go au naturel and not bother to primp? Popping a breath mint she'd dug for and found at the very bottom of her purse, she tried not to think about what she was doing.

Her slacks were wrinkled, but there was nothing she could do about that, short of borrowing an iron. Josh and Dolly and their new little daughter were still ensconced in the bedroom behind a closed door, from which Alex had barely heard a peep all night. She was resigned to being as fresh and neat as she was going to be till she got down the mountain and had a chance to take a shower at Irma's. In the meantime, she'd go back into the living room, sit by the window and watch the dawn till Spencer woke up.

She glanced once more at her reflection, chided herself for being a fool, then opened the door to see Spencer headed down the hall toward the bathroom...in his sweatshirt and boxers. The bathroom light spilled out and revealed the details of those boxers, which were black silk with orange pumpkins on them. Below the boxers were the longest, sexiest legs Alex had ever seen.

She gaped while Spencer continued to approach, apparently unaware of her presence. He was yawning, his head thrown back, his eyes momentarily closed. With an elbow in the air, he seemed to be trying to knead a kink out of the back of his neck.

Suddenly his eyes opened and he stopped in his tracks. But instead of apologizing and retreating to find his jeans and put them on, he smiled.

It was a lazy smile, morning-sexy…and lethal in its charm.

Chapter Eight

"Morning," he said, as if he were fully clothed and had every right to be conversational.

"Just barely," she murmured.

"Didn't think you were up yet."

"Obviously." Her gaze flicked to his boxers, then back to his face. She was glad she hadn't put on blush. Judging by the heat she felt in her cheeks, it would have been redundant.

That's when it finally dawned on him. He looked where she'd looked, discovered himself not fit for the company of a woman with whom he was determined to remain on strictly chaste terms, lost the grin and quickly returned to the living room. She heard some part of his body connect with an immovable object, a muted curse, and a hobbled continuation toward the spot where his jeans lay. She covered her mouth and giggled, then gave him time to get into his pants before returning to the living room.

Standing by a window, from which a gray light was now beginning to filter through the room, she kept her back carefully turned.

"Sorry about that," he mumbled. "I'm a little

groggy in the morning. Took me a moment to realize—''

''I understand. Just get ready to go so we can get out of here, okay?''

''I'm with you there,'' he said grimly.

She heard him leave the room and couldn't help an appreciative smile as she remembered how he'd looked in those gaudy boxers. Had a patient given him those, too, or was it just another facet of Spencer's personality coming to light? And what about that sexy, come-and-get-me smile? He'd evidently been groggy enough to forget not only his pants, but that the night before they'd made the agonizing decision not to have a steamy romance.

He returned in moments, his hair neatly combed, his movements and manners brisk and businesslike as he collected his medical bag and jacket. ''The sun's up and Red's crowing his head off. I think we can safely get down the mountain now. Ready?''

She sighed. His armor was in place and their magic night on the mountain was definitely at an end. She picked up her own jacket, purse and camera. ''Ready.''

The drive down the mountain was slow because the roads were as muddy as Josh had predicted they'd be, and Alex was glad they hadn't tried to travel them last night in the dark right after a drenching shower. But the awkwardness of the morning after a night of confessions and a shared kiss made the trip seem even longer. Alex was relieved when they finally pulled into Irma's driveway.

''I'll carry your suitcase inside,'' Spencer said.

''No. That's okay. I'm used to lugging my suitcase around,'' she quickly objected.

"I insist."

They both got out of the car and Alex opened the trunk. Spencer looked at the coat of mud that covered the entire car as a result of their overnight adventure and said, "I'll wash this for you later today."

"That's not necessary."

"I insist."

Spencer grabbed her suitcase and she followed him up the sidewalk to the porch and into the house. Although Irma had spent the night next door, the door was still unlocked.

"Which room? The one with the blue bedspread?"

Alex nodded, resigned to the fact that Spencer was going to be a gentleman to the end even if both of them wanted nothing more than to put distance between them. She followed him up the stairs, her gaze involuntarily lingering on those long legs of his, remembering how they'd looked minus the jeans.

In the bedroom, he set her suitcase down by the closet and turned. For the first time since she'd caught him in his underwear, they allowed themselves to look directly into each other's eyes. That's when Alex realized that, while they might be off the mountain, the magic was still there. Despite being sleep-deprived and unshowered, if he'd reached for her at that moment, she'd have been unable to resist. And the bed was so conveniently close...

"I've got to hurry and bathe and get out there with my camera while the light's good and the leaves are still wet from the rain," she blurted nervously.

"Right. I'll see you later," he said, sounding just as nervous. He walked quickly to the door, but stopped suddenly. Alex waited while he stood with his back to her for a full moment, her nerves taut, both fearful and hopeful that he really was going to take her into his arms.

Finally he turned just far enough to say over his shoulder, "If you can get back by nine, that's when Gran makes her regular Saturday morning pancake and sausage breakfast. We eat at my house. I know she'd want me to make sure you were invited."

Alex quietly released the breath she'd been holding. "I'll...I'll try to get back. But I can't be sure."

He nodded curtly, then left. It was only after she'd heard his quick footfalls on the stairs and the door shut behind him that she took another breath.

She sank to the edge of the bed and rested her elbows on her knees, staring at the floor. Of course she'd go to the breakfast. Her whole reason for coming to Jonesville was to see as much of her nieces as she could, especially in their home environment, interacting with their caregivers. This was the perfect opportunity.

But with Spencer there, she wondered if she'd even be able to remember her real reason for coming to Jonesville.

With another sigh, she got up and went into the bathroom, turning on the tap to fill the claw-foot tub. Maybe she could soak away her troubles, just like the bubble-bath TV commercial said she could.

Fat chance.

SPENCER WAS HOLDING Camilla Rose in his lap, reading to her from a book made out of glossy, cardboard pages. It was a story about a family of ducks and she loved the parts where he quacked, because she quacked, too. For such an active baby, she was surprisingly happy to be quietly held and read to, and had picked up a few sound effects as a result of this...the two most distinguishable being "quack" and "moo." There was no doubt that Camilla was smart as a whip. Just like her sisters.

He glanced up from the book and looked down the hall toward the kitchen where Lizzie and Maggie were helping Gran with breakfast. After a shower and shave, he'd come downstairs to find all three of them mixing batter and frying sausages. He'd told Gran about the Ford's new baby, expressing his undiminished awe at the miracle of birth, describing the tiny infant's fuzzy blond hair and delicate hands and feet. Lizzie and Maggie had been listening, enthralled, but as soon as he'd looked at them, they'd looked away, pretending to be uninterested.

How was he ever going to get through to them? What was it going to take to get them to accept him? Delivering the Ford's baby had just intensified his longing to be a real father to the girls.

Camilla banged impatiently on the book with her chubby, open palm, quacking loudly. Spencer looked down into her big blue eyes and chuckled. "All right. All right. I'm sorry, Camilla. I'll finish the story. I just got a little sidetracked."

Another interruption came in the form of the doorbell ringing. Spencer's heart gave a lurch. It was probably Alexandra. Lizzie and Maggie must have thought so, too, because they charged in from the kitchen to answer the door.

"Hi, girls," came Alexandra's friendly greeting from the entryway.

"Hi, Alex," they chirped in unison.

"We helped Gran make pancakes," Lizzie said. "Are you going to eat with us?

"*Please* eat with us," Maggie said.

As they entered the living room, Alexandra was laughing and holding on to both girls' hands. Or, probably, *they* were holding on to *her* hands. When she saw him her smile wavered for an instant, but she recovered quickly and said, "Hello."

"Hello," he returned, then politely inquired, "Did you get any good pictures?"

He wasn't sure what she replied because he was too busy trying to hide and moderate his reaction to seeing her. The sexual and emotional tension between them when he'd carried her suitcase up to Gran's guest room had nearly done him in and he had to make sure he was never alone with her like that again. He'd been far too optimistic to believe that admitting their attraction to each other would help. Apparently he was doomed to be just as enchanted by this woman as the girls were.

She was dressed casually today in jeans, a dark green turtleneck sweater and black suede ankle boots. She'd carried in a black pea jacket, which she laid on a nearby chair. But she could be wearing a gunnysack and he'd think she looked sexy. Her hair wasn't as girlishly curly as it had been that morning, but the smoother, more sophisticated look suited her just as well. Hell, everything suited her.

"So, I figured I deserved a break and thought I'd stop by for some of those delicious pancakes of Irma's," she was saying by the time Spencer started paying attention again. She looked around the room. "This is a nice house. It's very similar to your grandmother's, isn't it? Inside and out."

"Yeah, well, the same builder—"

"Are you coming to the festival, Alex?" Lizzie interrupted, tugging on her hand. "Do you want to see my costume? Do *you* have a costume?"

"I'm going as Snow White," Maggie confided excitedly.

"And I'm going as Cinderella," Lizzie added proudly. "Maybe you could be Sleeping Beauty or Belle from *Beauty and the Beast*. You could come with us!"

"What's your dad going to be?" Alexandra asked, tactfully trying to include Spencer in the conversation.

Maggie turned and peered from under her lashes at him, but Lizzie didn't even spare him a glance, saying with a shrug of her shoulders, "Oh, if you're talking about Dr. Jones, I don't know what costume *he's* wearing. And he's *not* our dad."

Alexandra's expression was one of alarm and apology. She couldn't help it that the girls had taken to her so quickly while still pretending that he didn't exist, but Spencer also couldn't help feeling jealous and hurt. And desperate. So desperate, in fact...

He stood up abruptly. "Girls, take Camilla and go into the kitchen."

Lizzie and Maggie stared at him. So did Alexandra. No one moved.

"I *said*...take Camilla and go into the kitchen, please. Alex and I will be there in a minute. There's something we need to talk about first."

Lizzie glared at him. She obviously wanted to argue, but that would require speaking to him. Maggie looked distressed, and Camilla, feeling the tension in the room, started to whimper.

"*Now,* Elizabeth."

Lizzie squared her jaw and got a mulish look on her pretty face, but she did as she was told. Spencer put Camilla on the floor and Lizzie took her hand and pulled her into the kitchen almost too fast for the poor little thing's toddling legs to keep up. Maggie lagged behind them, glancing over her shoulder at Spencer and Alexandra with a woebegone look that tugged at his heart.

"What was that all about?" Alexandra asked him as soon as the girls were out of earshot. "You're not usually so short with them, are you?"

He cupped her elbow and urged her ahead of him down the hall toward the library. "Of course not. I hate making them unhappy. But would you blame me if I was a little short with them occasionally? They treat me like I'm an especially disgusting strain of bacteria."

When they got to the den, Alexandra pulled free and frowned up at him. "This isn't going to be another honesty session, is it? You and I both know that the last one didn't work."

"This isn't about us, if that's what you're worried about. It's about the girls."

"The girls have been through a lot. You need to be more patient."

"I've been patient for nearly three months, Alex. Things aren't getting better, they're getting worse. And that fact's been clearer than ever to me since you showed up."

Her chin lifted. Her expression was wary. "What's that supposed to mean?"

"It means, when they're with you I see how sweet and open they can be. I see how much love they have to give...how much love they *want* to give. And I'm so damned jealous I could put a fist through the wall."

Alex was as torn as she'd ever felt in her life. She was filled with sympathy for Spencer, but she couldn't forget her father in this mess. He wanted the girls, too, and loyalty to her father demanded that she set aside any sympathy she felt for Spencer...didn't it? She was so confused!

She should just consider what was best for the girls, she told herself firmly. But that had become a confusing issue, too. She no longer felt she knew what was best for the girls.

"Will you help me, Alex?"

Alex blinked, then repeated stupidly, "Help you?"

"Gran's tried and Bernice has tried, but neither of them has gotten to square one talking to the girls about why they won't accept me. They just clam up as soon as my name is mentioned. At the risk of being frozen out, too, they've had to back off. You wouldn't need to worry about that risk. You aren't going to be a permanent part of their lives."

And Bernice is? For some reason, Bernice's inclusion and her exclusion from the Jones family circle got Alex's hackles up. She was their aunt, for crying out loud!

Controlling her irritation with an effort, she inquired, "What about talking to a child psychiatrist? Have you done that? As a doctor yourself, surely you know a specialist who might be able to give you some insight into the girls' behavior.''

Spencer shoved his hands into the pockets of his corduroy pants and sat down on the edge of a massive mahogany desk that fit in perfectly with the rest of the manly decor in the librarylike room he'd dragged her to. Impatiently he replied, ''Of course I've talked to some of my colleagues and I've got theories and insight coming out of my ears. I've got some theories of my own, too, but no way to address the problem if the girls won't talk about it...to me or to anyone. I feel certain we could solve this problem if they'd only *talk* to me.''

Alex figured she'd risk getting her head bit off, but she had to ask, ''Have you ever considered that maybe...you know, just *maybe*... you ought to let the girls' grandfather have them? That maybe they just need to be with their real family?''

He was angry, no doubt about it. She could tell by the way his jaw tensed and his eyes smoldered. But he held his anger in check admirably. ''They *are* with their real family. At least—'' He stood up, took his hands out of his pockets to shove up the sleeves of his navy-blue cardigan pullover and paced the rug in front of a small fireplace. ''It's what Karlie wanted. Karlie *and* Richard.''

Since they were on the subject and he was already angry with her, she figured she might as well go for broke. ''Which strikes me as very odd. Haven't you ever thought that it was strange that an old girlfriend you hadn't seen in six years, and even her husband—a man I've heard was very proud and arrogant—wanted you to raise their daughters? You and not their own grandfather?''

He stopped pacing and faced her. His expression was implacable. "No. No, I haven't wondered, because I *know* why they wanted me to raise the girls. Karlie left me a letter. She explained."

She waited. She was dying to ask him what the letter said. It was the sixty-four-thousand-dollar question that had plagued her ever since hearing about it. If she only knew what the letter said, she'd understand why Karlie and Richard had chosen a guardian outside the family. And if she understood, maybe she could accept the way things were. And maybe she could convince her father to accept the way things were.

It seemed Spencer had partly read her mind. "It doesn't matter what the letter said, Alex. Besides, its contents were meant for only me to read. Suffice it to say, Karlie convinced me that taking the girls was the right thing for them. For them *and* for me. Let's leave it at that."

But Alex couldn't leave it at that. An idea that had presented itself before, an idea that would explain why he'd do anything Karlie asked, came forcefully to mind. "Have you been in love with her all these years?"

"No. No, I haven't. I have fond memories of our time together, but it's in the past. I haven't been in love with Karlie for over five years."

His answer was so immediate and matter-of-fact, Alex believed him. And for some reason, for a reason she didn't dare analyze too closely, she was profoundly relieved.

There was a light tapping on the door, followed by Irma's entrance into the room with a concerned expression on her usually cheerful face. "What's going on, Spence? Elizabeth and Margaret are sulking to beat the band and Camilla's crying her eyes out, calling for Daddy and quacking at the same time.''

''I'm sorry, Gran. I was talking to Alex about the girls. I just thought she might be able to help me to—'' He suddenly seemed to realize what she'd said. ''She's calling for Daddy?''

Gran smiled. ''She sure is. I believe it's her first real word. Can't really count 'quack' or 'moo,' can we?''

Spencer beamed. ''Not if you ask me.'' He turned to Alex. ''I'd better go. I hate it when she cries. But think about what we've talked about, Alex. I know you barely know me and the girls. You're not here to get involved in our problems and you have your own work to do, but you just might be able to help. Think about it. I'd be eternally grateful if you could just convince those little girls to give me half a chance. I want us to be a family more than anything in the world.''

He left the room, and left Alex in a state of overwhelming confusion and emotional chaos. She looked at Irma, who was studying her with a sympathetic expression.

''He's not asking a lot, is he?'' she said wryly. ''But don't fret, Alex. If you don't think you can help, Spencer will understand. He just sees the rapport you have with the girls and will try anything he can to get some results.''

''What do you think, Irma?'' Alex asked her. ''Do you think I might be able to get the girls to at least talk to him? And, even if I did, do you think it would resolve the problem of their not accepting him?''

''I don't know. And you won't know, either, unless you try. I figure it can't hurt. I think they'll warm to him eventually, but sooner's better than later. This is hard on Spence, and he's a good man...even though I do say so myself and I'm his grandmother. You do have an uncanny rapport with the girls, as if they've known and trusted you forever instead of just meeting you for the first time yesterday. You truly might be able to help. But it's up to you, Alex.'' She whisked her hands together as if she was through with the subject and smiled. ''Come on into the kitchen and have some pancakes. No one can think clearly on an empty stomach.''

Alex followed Irma into the kitchen, an updated room with pristine white cabinets and a laminated wood floor. The girls and Spencer were sitting around a country-style pine table. Camilla sat in Spencer's lap and he was helping her to a drink of orange juice, her tears forgotten now that ''Daddy'' was holding her. Elizabeth and Margaret were sulking, just as Irma had reported, but their faces lit up when she entered the room.

Breakfast progressed much as dinner had the night before, with the girls begging for Alex's attention and talking her ears off while ignoring Spencer. By the end of the meal she had promised to meet them at the festival in time for an early dinner at five, followed by participation in the Halloween costume contest.

When she and Irma stood to leave, their first destination to be Irma's attic to hunt for appropriate Halloween attire, she hardly knew what expression to put on her face when she looked at Spencer. His expression was neutral, but his eyes held a wealth of meaning. She left, shaken and confused and wanting more than anything to call her father and pour out every doubt and feeling in her heart.

While rummaging through the trunks and boxes in the attic for the next half hour, Irma never once brought up the subject of Spencer's plea for help. She simply kept up a cheerful conversation while tossing vintage clothes at Alex to try on. Alex's distracted and halfhearted participation finally prompted Irma to say, "Look, hon, I'll put something together for you and lay it out on your bed. You trust me, don't you?"

"Of course, Irma. It really doesn't matter what I wear anyway."

"Posh! Of course it matters. The girls'll be disappointed if you don't do something kind of fun. They'd go nuts if you won the contest. Now go take your pictures or wander in the woods or do whatever you think'll make you feel better and get you in the party mood for tonight."

"Thank you, Irma," Alex said gratefully. "You're a sweetheart. You're sure you don't mind?"

She flicked her wrists at Alex. "Scoot, now. I've got a prizewinning costume to put together."

Alex left the house, hopped in her clean car—the mud had disappeared while she was in the attic, the work of a man who probably religiously kept his word—and drove to the nearest phone booth. Settled inside with the midmorning Autumn sun beating on the glass, she dialed her father's cell phone number. He was always after her to carry one herself, but cell phones usually weren't much use in the foreign far-reaches she frequented.

After three rings, he answered.

"Ethington."

"Dad?"

His voice immediately warmed. "Hi, Lex! Where are you, sweetheart? Is everything okay? When will you be home?"

She laughed. "Hey, one question at a time. First, where are *you?* You're not on the freeway, are you? I don't want to distract you while you're driving at eighty miles an hour."

"I'm at the club having a drink."

"What kind of drink?"

"It's only ten-thirty in the morning, Lex. I'm having mineral water with a spritz of lime. That okay, prissy miss?" he teased.

"Just checking on you."

"Don't worry. You convinced me to take care of myself despite everything that's going on. Where are you calling from? My caller ID says Pay Phone."

"I'm all over the place, Dad. Mostly in the wilds of New England. I'm taking pictures for a nature magazine, remember?"

"Couldn't be too wild if there's a pay phone. But that's fine by me. How's it going? Got some good pictures?"

She thought of the pictures she'd taken of Camilla's first steps and of Spencer holding the Ford's newborn baby in his big, capable hands. "Yep. I've got some *great* pictures."

"Then you're coming home soon?"

"Not till Monday. I just needed to talk to you, Dad."

"Is something wrong?" The immediate concern in his voice touched her. "Tell me, Lex."

Yes, everything's wrong. I've got myself in a terrible mess and I'm going to end up hurting you or hurting some other people I've grown surprisingly fond of in less than twenty-four hours.

She thought all this, but only said, "Nothing's wrong. I just miss you."

"Well, I miss you, too, pumpkin, but you're usually gone for months at a time. Why're you suddenly so sentimental and missing your old dad after just a couple of days?"

"It's just that I've been thinking about the situation with Richard's little girls and, well…"

"Yes?" he prompted eagerly. "What have you been thinking? Have you figured out a sure-fire way to get them back where they belong?"

"No. No, I haven't." Her throat ached and her cheeks burned, but she forced herself to say the words she knew would hurt and confuse him. "In fact, I was wondering if maybe it would be…well…better just to leave them where they are."

There was dead silence on the other end of the line.

"Dad, you still there?"

"Yes, I'm still here. I'm just a little surprised." There was another long pause, then, quietly, "How come you've changed your mind all of a sudden?"

"It's not *that* sudden," she said. "It's something I've had in the back of my mind for a while."

When he didn't respond, she forged on. "I know you love them and want them with you, and I understand that. But what if they're happy where they are? What if Spencer…what if this Dr. Jones person loves them as much as you do? They've been with him nearly three months, you know. Wouldn't it be traumatic if they had to pack up and move again in a few months—or a few years, depending on how long it takes—if you win the custody battle?''

Again her father was silent. This time she waited till he was ready to talk again. Finally he said in a voice that clearly showed his astonishment, pain and confusion. ''I don't know what to say, Lex. Only I'm not sure you really do understand how I feel about this. But maybe it's just trying to talk over the phone that's got us at cross-purposes. Why don't you tell me exactly where you are and I'll fly out there to meet you? My plane's always ready to go. We can talk better in person.''

She shook her head, tears springing to her eyes. She'd accomplished nothing constructive by calling her father. She'd only perplexed and hurt him and made her own conflicts harder to resolve. ''No, Dad. I've still got a lot of work to do. We'll talk on Monday.''

''Okay.'' His tone was doubtful, hesitant. ''You'll call me as soon as you get in?''

''I promise. I love you, Dad. And…and I'm sorry.''

''Sorry about what, Lex? Honey, what's going—''

''Goodbye, Dad.''

She quickly hung up the phone and roughly wiped her cheeks free of tears. It was then that she realized she'd already made up her mind what to do about the girls. She was going to do what Spencer had asked her to do. She was going to talk to them and see if they'd give their new dad a chance.

She knew in her heart it was the right thing to do. They were settled in a home, a *good* home, and it would be a shame to uproot them again. She just hoped that if she was really able to bring Spencer and the girls together as a family, she'd still have a family of her own to go home to. That her father, the father she'd lived without for the first fifteen years of her life, would understand and forgive her.

Chapter Nine

Alex spent the afternoon in the woods taking pictures and thinking, then began the drive back to Irma's house at four o'clock to change into her costume. She was still resolved to talk to the girls, see if she could help them become—as Spencer had expressed—part of a "real family."

But her heart ached for her father and worried about how he was going to feel toward her once he knew what she'd done. He'd turned to her for help to get the girls back. Now, especially if she was successful in getting Elizabeth and Margaret to talk to and accept Spencer as their daddy, she would be working to keep them exactly where they were.

The only thing that consoled her at all was the hope that down the road, once everything had settled down and emotions weren't so raw, Spencer would agree to allow her father to be part of the girls' lives. She'd like to be part of the girls' lives, too, but she doubted that Spencer could forgive her when he found out she was Richard's half sister and had only come to Jonesville to gather evidence to support her father's custody suit. And he would find out eventually...after she was gone.

She'd got herself in a real mess, that was for sure. Inevitably she was going to make both of the important men in her life very angry with her.

When she got to the house, she wasn't sure when Irma's friend was bringing her car back, so she parked in front, halfway between Irma's house and Spencer's. After she killed the engine, she just sat there for a minute wondering how on earth Spencer Jones had become, in so short a time, an important man in her life. She shook her head, got out and went inside. She didn't bother to knock or announce herself because she knew Irma was already at the Harvest Festival with Spencer and the girls.

She climbed the stairs, still deep in thought, and went into her room...a room she hadn't even slept in yet! She dropped her camera, purse and jacket on a chair and moved to the bed to see what sort of an outfit Irma had been able to throw together for her.

Her jaw dropped. The gown laid out for her was exquisite, Victorian style with a Spanish flavor. It was a vivid jade-green, floor-length with a cinched-in waist, puffed sleeves that ended at the elbows in a drape of elegant black lace, a scooped neckline, and row after row of black ruffles peeking through a parted skirt in the front.

There were accessories, too. A black velvet choker with an ornate silver charm shaped like a rose, dangle earrings of the same style, and a fancy black filigreed comb that could be set atop one's head like a tiara. There was even a black shawl with an elegant fringe at least six inches wide that would come in quite handy as the temperatures cooled off that evening.

Did any female ever outgrow the desire to play

dress-up? Alex wondered as she picked up the gown and held it against her, swaying this way and that in front of a full-length mirror by the door. Elizabeth had said she was going to the festival dressed as Cinderella, but that's exactly who Alex felt like as she admired her reflection and grinned uncontrollably. Certainly only a fairy godmother could have come up with such a perfect gown in such a short time. And if it actually fit her, Alex would be convinced that magic was involved!

She quickly pulled off her boots, jeans and sweater and slipped the gown over her head. The fabric did not look or feel like a fragile antique—in fact she suspected it was an exceptionally deceptive polyester—so she doubted that Irma had gotten the dress out of the attic. Besides, it had a zipper in the back. Where *did* she get it?

It fit! She couldn't believe it! She stared at herself in the mirror, wishing she hadn't cut her hair. She'd have looked like a real *señorita* from the nineteenth century with long hair to set off the beauty of the comb Irma had provided. But no amount of wishing was going to make her hair grow back by the time she left for the festival, she reminded herself ruefully.

Alex carefully removed the gown and laid it lovingly on the bed again, then headed for the bathroom. A dress like that deserved to be worn only by a woman who'd bathed in scented bubbles and primped till she felt as beautiful as the clothes she was wearing.

She wondered if the girls would like her costume. After all, it wasn't a recognizable character like their costumes. Then, as she dumped a healthy dollop of rose-scented bubble-bath under the running tap, she wondered what Spencer would think of it....

Forty-five minutes later, Alex was hurrying down the street toward the town square, her camera hidden under the drape of her shawl. She'd driven by earlier that day and had been delighted at the sight of the colorful booths and tents scattered over the green that fanned out from the central focal point of a white-steepled church, the whole effect set off by scattered trees sporting red and yellow leaves. And now, just as Spencer had predicted, the whole town seemed to have turned out for the festivities. She saw a lot of costumes, mostly on the children, but saw nothing she liked better than the costume Irma had conjured up for her.

Irma had told her to meet them at the main eating area where there were picnic tables under a bowery, adjacent to a temporary stage constructed just for the festival. As she walked through the crowd she could smell roasting corn on the cob and barbecued meat wafting on the air. Apparently she was going in the right direction!

But first she had to pass a lot of booths doing brisk business, and many crowds around tables where jam, pie and cake tasting contests were being conducted. The community spirit and the simple, down-home fun of it all was like nothing she'd ever seen or experienced before. She hadn't even met up with her party yet and she was already having a wonderful time!

Then, just as she spied the picnic tables a few yards away, she came across the statue of the founding father, Josiah Jones, around which the town square was situated. She stared up at the statue, arrested by the stunning genetic similarities that had been passed down through so many generations from Dr. Josiah Jones to Dr. Spencer Jones. They had the same lanky height, same lean face, same beautiful, capable hands. Just looking at the statue made Alex's insides flutter.

Dragging her fascinated gaze away from the statue, she headed once again toward the bowery. Finally she reached the picnic tables about ten minutes after five and scanned the crowd for Spencer, Irma and the girls. Suddenly she saw a pint-size Cinderella and Snow White running toward her.

"We thought you weren't coming," Elizabeth exclaimed, out of breath as she clutched Alex's hand. "Where were you?"

"Yeah, where *were* you?" Margaret echoed.

As she looked into the girls' faces, she realized that they'd really been worried that she wouldn't show up. They were smiling now, but there was still a trace of anxiousness in their voices, a look of lingering nervousness in their eyes. These little girls were obviously still insecure from the loss of their parents and Alex made a solemn vow in that moment that she would never again purposely set out to undermine the security they were building in their new home.

"I'm sorry I'm late. It took me a while to get into my costume," she told them cheerfully. "How do you like it?"

The girls looked her over, wide-eyed, saying nothing. She laughed when she realized they probably didn't have the slightest idea who she was supposed to be unless they'd watched a video of *Zorro* lately.

"Wow, you look pretty. Are you some kind of princess?" Margaret asked her.

"No, silly," Elizabeth chided her with a giggle. "She's a Spanish *señorita!*"

Surprised, Alex exclaimed, "Elizabeth, how'd you know what I—"

But before Alex could get the question out, she saw Irma approaching in a witch outfit, complete with a green face and a hairy wart on her nose big enough to be seen from several feet away. She was carrying Camilla Rose, who was dressed adorably as a duck and was making quacking noises as she bounced on Irma's hip. They were accompanied by Bernice, pigtailed and perky as Dorothy from the *Wizard of Oz,* and Spencer...

Dressed as Zorro.

Several thoughts flashed through Alex's mind at once.

Irma had obviously purposely put together a costume for her that "went" with Spencer's. But why? Could Spencer's grandmother possibly be indulging in a little matchmaking?

What would Bernice think?

What would *Spencer* think?

But, despite the importance of these considerations, Alex found herself unable to concentrate on anything but the way Spencer looked in that costume.

The tight-fitting pants.

The shiny, knee-high boots.

The cape.

The dashing hat.

All in deep, dark, delicious black.

And... *the mask.*

The black mask, contoured to the chiseled angles of his lean face, fascinated and beguiled her most of all. It accentuated two features she'd found alarmingly attractive even before he'd put on the mask…his eyes and his mouth. Piercing blue twinkled mischievously at her through those mask slits, and a rueful smile tilted his sensuously molded lips.

"*Señorita,*" he said with a playfully gallant bow. "Have we met before?"

Alex smiled back and curtsied. In her best Spanish accent, she replied, "I believe you may have rescued me once or twice…Zorro."

Alex was completely spellbound by the way Spencer's eyes crinkled behind the mask and the way his teeth looked as white as a matinee idol's as they shared a laugh. But their absorption in each other was abruptly brought to a halt when Bernice spoke.

"How did you know Spencer was going as Zorro?" she inquired coldly. "He said he didn't tell anyone. He didn't even tell *me* what he was wearing. Did…did he tell *you?*"

Alex looked at Bernice, saw equal parts of hurt and hostility in her expression, then looked at Irma, whose expression remained neutral. Alex didn't want to place the blame on Irma, so she tried to talk around the truth without actually lying.

"Spencer didn't tell me that he was coming as Zorro. Honestly, Bernice, I didn't know. I was just as surprised as you that my costume seems to…complement his."

At the conclusion of this speech, Bernice was still frowning. Now she turned and looked up at Spencer.

"I didn't tell Alex who I was coming as," he said truthfully. "I didn't tell anyone."

He hadn't had to tell Irma, who was, undoubtedly, the person who'd helped him put together his costume, just as she'd helped Alex with hers. But Bernice was smart enough to figure that out for herself. She transferred her confused and accusing gaze to Irma.

Irma looked uncomfortable, but admitted to nothing. Again, Alex wondered why Irma had done such a thing. Why would she intentionally upset Bernice?

The little girls had apparently picked up on the tension between the grown-ups. Camilla Rose stopped quacking and reached for Spencer, whining. He took her from Gran and sat her on his arm, then she buried her face in his neck. Elizabeth clutched harder than ever to Alex's hand, and Margaret hid in the folds of Irma's voluminous black skirt.

Alex felt guilty for causing problems, but she hadn't done it intentionally.

"Let's go sit down, Bernice," Spencer said soothingly. "The kids are hungry and so am I. How about you? Want me to bring you some corn on the cob?"

"I'm not hungry, Spence," Bernice said in a tone of hurt dignity. "In fact, I feel restless and think I'll walk around and look at the booths and exhibits for a while."

After a hesitation that Alex knew would do nothing to help convince Bernice of his eagerness, Spencer said, "Do you want me to come with you? I'll come with you if you want."

It was a gesture that came too little, too late. "No, Spence. I don't want you to come with me." She forced a tight smile for the girls' benefit. "See you later, Elizabeth, Margaret."

"Bye, Bernice," they said in unison.

She turned and strode away in her red, glitter-speckled high heels, the basket on her arm with a stuffed Toto inside tucked against her hip, her head held high. She didn't bother to say "boo" to the rest of them.

Spencer turned to Irma. *"Gran...."*

"Say, girls, let's go pile up some plates with a bunch of that good smelling grub," Irma said. "Your dad and Alex can take Camilla and find us a table where we'll all fit." She looked Spencer square in the eye and said quietly, "I know you want to talk, Spence. But let's do it later, okay? We're here to have some family fun."

Spencer nodded curtly. Irma nodded back, took the two girls' hands and walked away toward the smoking barbecue grills.

"I'll bring you back a plate, Alex," Elizabeth called over her shoulder.

"Me, too!" Margaret added.

"So, you get two plates and I get squat," Spencer remarked, but his tone wasn't sarcastic or angry, just resigned.

"Oh, Spencer, I don't know what to say," Alex said, truly appalled by the hubbub she'd started by just showing up. "Not about the girls' behavior or your grandmother's. What do you think possessed her to dress me up to look like your romantic match? Especially when she knew we'd all be hanging out together...including Bernice?"

"It isn't like Gran to intentionally cause trouble," Spencer said grimly. "But, like she said, we're here to have fun and I don't want to ruin things for the girls, so I'll get the story from her later.''

"Haven't I already ruined things by making Bernice walk off in a huff?''

"You didn't hear the girls complain when she left, did you?'' he said ruefully. "That probably rankled her, too.'' He rubbed Camilla's back and kissed her forehead. She immediately started quacking again.

"Poor Bernice,'' he continued. "It didn't help that the girls have talked of nothing except you all day. And hearing that you and I had spent the night together up on the mountain—''

"How did she find out about that?''

"I told her, of course.''

"Of course,'' Alex repeated with a sigh. "You and your honesty thing.''

A family walked by and called greetings to Spencer. Although he looked a little distracted at first, he obviously liked the family. He introduced Alex to Pete and Kathy Anderson and about a half-dozen kids, all in their teens. Despite the fact that she already had enough children for a team and she looked at least forty, the woman was pregnant and glowing. After the Andersons moved on, a couple of giggling teenage girls passed and waved, saying in a flirtatious singsong, "Hello, Dr. Jones.'' He waved and smiled perfunctorily, then turned back to Alex, picking up right where he left off.

"Then, to top it all, you showed up looking like—'' He broke off and gestured at her outfit, then finished with, "Well, like *that*.''

Alex self-consciously clutched the shawl closer around her, amazed at how the Cinderella transformation that had filled her with such delight just an hour ago could now make her feel so miserable. She bent her head and stared at her boots peeking out from the hem of her "magical" gown.

A shock thrilled through her, though, as Spencer touched her arm. She looked up into his eyes—eyes that were so incredibly mesmerizing with the mask to set them off—and saw apology and tenderness in his expression.

"No, Alex. Don't do that. Don't try to cover up. None of this is your fault. And the costume is perfect on you." His voice lowered and grew husky. "You look beautiful, Alex. Absolutely irresistible."

She felt herself blushing. Her body suffused with heat from head to toe. She couldn't help but respond to his tender smile with a smile of her own. "Thank you, Spencer." Then, shyly, "You don't look half bad yourself."

Boy, what a dumb understatement! Alex thought. But Spencer's grin seemed to indicate that he was pleased with the small compliment. Heck, if she told him what she really thought of his costume—that it made her want to wrestle him to the ground and make steamy romance-novel love to him on the spot—it would either embarrass him, or inspire him to make steamy romance-novel love to her, too!

Thank goodness Camilla broke the tension with an especially loud chorus of quacks just then. They both laughed, then Spencer asked, as he bounced his baby daughter on his slim, black-sheathed hip, "Think I've got a shot at winning the costume contest?"

"Well, if the women judges are in the majority, I'd say you can't lose," Alex admitted. "Especially if you take Camilla up there with you. You're a dose of dangerous sexuality in that head-to-toe black, and a darling daddy-figure to boot, Dr. Jones.''

''Well, I don't know about that,'' he replied modestly, but was obviously very pleased with her answer. ''I'd say *you're* a sure winner, though.''

Alex shook her head firmly, immediately sober. ''Oh, I'm not going to enter the contest, Spencer. To promenade on stage in front of the whole town in an outfit that clearly goes with yours—as if we were a couple!—would be a real slap in the face to Bernice. Things will be hard enough for her already. I'm sure people will be asking her all kinds of questions about me.''

Spencer frowned and bounced Camilla a little more hectically. She'd started to squirm, wanting to get down. ''You're right. I didn't even think of how your entering the contest would affect Bernice. Trouble is, lately I haven't been thinking at all of Bernice *or* her feelings.'' He paused, seemed to consider, then added, ''All I can think about is you.''

As thrilled as she was by what Spencer had just said, Alex felt duty-bound to answer reasonably. ''Spencer, you know you shouldn't even say that to me. We discussed this on the mountain. You said you had compelling reasons not to get involved with me, and Bernice and a possible future with her was the most compelling reason of all, so—''

''I know what I said while we were up on the mountain,'' he interrupted, but then was approached by another couple who would have stopped to talk if he hadn't turned away after a friendly but quick hello.

He grabbed Alex's elbow and pulled her out of

the traffic to under a tree a few feet away from the picnic tables, then continued. "I thought I was being so damned up-front when I insisted on that little talk, but I was just saying what I wished were true. I know now that I can never have a future with Bernice...and it has nothing and *everything* to do with you!"

Alex bowed her head and bit her lip. She wasn't prepared for more of Spencer's honesty. She didn't deserve his honesty.

"I suppose we could never have had a relationship, Alex, even without Bernice in the picture, because you've got that glamorous globe-trotting career and a fiancé. But just the fact that I can feel about you the way I do proves I can never marry Bernice. I'll never feel this way about her—the way I feel about you in just two days—and that wouldn't be fair to her or to me. I've come to realize that I want more than a mother for my children...I want a wife I can love with my whole soul. And if I never find a woman I can feel that way about who'll marry me, then I'll stay a bachelor. The girls won't suffer, though, because I intend to be the best single father in the world. No, I won't even qualify it. I won't say best *single* father. I'm going to be the best father in the world to my three girls."

There was no doubt in Alex's mind that he would do just that...and she was going to help him while she still could, while he still liked and trusted her. Before he knew who she really was and how deceptive she'd been. Emotion had gathered in her throat and was nearly choking her, but she had no time for regret or sentiment. She would talk to the girls, talk about Spencer as if she was the president of his fan club, then she'd get out of his life before she made an even bigger mess of it.

He had set Camilla on the ground and was holding her hands while she "waddled" around in her fuzzy duck costume.

"About me talking to the girls..."

He looked up abruptly, "Alex, please forget I asked you to do that. It was presumptuous of me, but I was desperate. I completely understand you not wanting to get involved in our family matters."

"But I *do* want to get involved, Spencer."

He straightened up, lifting Camilla to his hip again. She couldn't mistake his look of cautious hope as he asked, "You do?"

"What I mean is, I'd like to see if I can help out before I...before I go," she hurriedly explained.

She saw the flicker of hope extinguish with her words. "I thought you were going to be around for several days?"

"I'm getting my work done a lot faster than I thought I would. I plan to leave tomorrow."

"Tomorrow?" he repeated, obviously dismayed.

"But that still gives me the rest of today and part of tomorrow to find an opportunity to talk to the girls. When would you suggest?"

He seemed to still be absorbing the shock that she'd be leaving so soon. She felt as sick about it as he appeared to, but it was the best thing for both of them.

"Spencer?"

He pulled himself together and said, "Alex, I hope you know how much I appreciate this."

She forced a laugh. "Hey, don't thank me yet. It may come to nothing."

"Considering how smitten they are with you, I doubt that very much. Anyway, you promised to read them a story, so how about taking your chances tonight at bedtime?"

She nodded. "Sounds perfect…as long as we don't keep them out too late. I don't want them falling asleep in the middle of my speech."

"May I ask what you plan to say?"

She smiled. "No, you may not. You're just going to have to trust me."

And in this case he could, she thought.

Their conference ended when the girls and Irma showed up with plates of food on a couple of trays. Spencer apologized for not finding a table as they'd been commissioned to do, but quickly set about the task and found a table they could all fit at, which was luckily quite close to the stage. They wouldn't have to budge once the program began because they had what amounted to front-row seats.

Alex firmly put her feelings for Spencer aside and concentrated all her attention on the girls and having fun with them. Even with Elizabeth and Margaret ignoring Spencer, they managed to have a lot of laughs over dinner and enjoyed a very tasty meal. She took a lot of pictures, too, painfully aware that the images she'd develop in her darkroom might be the only lasting evidence of this happy time with Spencer and the girls.

In consideration of the children involved, the costume contest began at the early hour of six. Gran and Alex convinced Elizabeth and Margaret to take their turn parading across the stage despite a last-minute fit of shyness. They didn't win the contest, but they didn't seem to mind. They giggled and clapped just as enthusiastically as everyone else when the tiny girl dressed as a ladybug took first prize in the Females Under Five category. Camilla Rose might have had a shot at the prize if she could have been persuaded to participate, but Spencer wisely didn't force her when she screamed bloody-murder the minute she was placed on the stage.

When the adult costume contest began, Spencer left to take his place with the people lined up to go on stage. Alex held a drowsy Camilla Rose and looked for Bernice, finally seeing her standing in the line next to a tall man dressed as Gumby. She was hanging onto his arm and flirting as if her life depended on it! Well, thought Alex, it looked like Bernice was giving Spencer what she figured he deserved…payback!

Alex leaned toward Gran. "Who's that Gumby guy with Bernice?"

"His name is Leonard Steinfeldt. He owns the gas station just off the highway as you're coming into town. He just moved here a few months ago and he's had a thing for Bernice since he first clapped eyes on her. He's shy, though, and by the time he got around to asking her out, she'd already started dating Spencer."

"And he probably figured he didn't have a snow-ball's chance in you know where against the local most eligible bachelor, right?"

Gran nodded sagely, glancing around to make sure the girls, who were busy consuming caramel candy apples, weren't listening. "Right. But it's my opinion that if Spencer hadn't taken notice of Bern-ice, she'd be married to Leonard by now. And it's also my opinion that Spencer would have lost interest in Bernice after the first couple of dates if he hadn't suddenly inherited a family of little females he thinks need a mother. Whether he realizes it or not, I think he's courtin' Bernice for the girls' sake, not for his. And if that's the case, it's not fair to her or to him. They'll never be truly happy.''

''I'm pretty sure Spencer realizes that now,'' Alex confided impetuously. She figured Irma deserved to know something about her grandson that might make her worry less about him. ''He said he's looking for a woman he can love heart and soul, not just someone who would fill the bill adequately as mother and wife.''

Irma's eyebrows shot sky-high. ''Well, praise be! Can you tell me what brought on this epiphany...or do I already know?''

''Don't press your grandmother-of-the-groom gown just yet, Irma,'' Alex warned her with a rueful smile. ''Spencer and I are *not* an item and will certainly never get married. So, if that's what you were hoping, I guess you wasted your effort on this costume. Although, I've certainly enjoyed it. It's beautiful. Where'd you get it?''

''I'm part of a group of old ladies who sew costumes for the community theater hereabouts and this afternoon I remembered this hot little number from our production of *Showboat*. Just a few added doodads made it look Spanish. That's where I got the outfit, but now back to your little speech about you and Spencer not being an item. Hmph! I'll bet you thought you'd got my mind off the subject, but no such luck, girly. 'Fess up. I've seen the way you two look at each other.''

''Looking is as far as it's going to go, Irma.''

"But—"

"No buts. Spencer will find the right woman eventually. It's just not going to be me." She patted Irma's arm consolingly. "Here's some news you're going to like, though. I've decided to talk to the girls tonight when it's time for their bedtime story. Maybe I'll be able to get through to them just enough to pave the way for Spencer to work his own charm…which we both know he has in abundance. All that's needed is a crack in their armor. Then it won't take long after that before they're calling him Daddy and talking his ears off."

"It's that first crack we've been waiting and praying for," Irma agreed. "No one around here has been able to put even a chink in Elizabeth's armor, and we all know she's the stubborn one telling Margaret what to do. Karlie had a stubborn streak, as I recall, and in that way Elizabeth's a lot like her mother."

"You didn't know her father. Maybe she got the stubbornness from him," Alex couldn't resist adding. If Irma had known Richard, she wouldn't hesitate to attribute most of Elizabeth's negative traits to her father.

Irma got a guarded look on her face and didn't answer, which Alex thought was uncharacteristic of Spencer's talkative and opinionated grandmother. But maybe, since she didn't actually know Elizabeth's father, she was unwilling to hazard a guess about whether or not he was stubborn.

It came as no surprise to anyone when Spencer won the contest. The hoots and hollers and whistles when he was on stage might have turned to boos and the throwing of rotten fruit if the judges hadn't picked him. But Alex thought he deserved to win on his own merit, not just because he was popular. Standing on that stage in his Zorro costume, she also thought he deserved *People* magazine's annual recognition of the Sexiest Man Alive.

It was obvious he was embarrassed, but Irma had explained that Spencer had entered the contest this year for the first time because several patients had agreed to donate money to the local Women's Shelter and Toys For Tots if he participated. Naturally this only increased Alex's respect for the man.

Damn. A good and decent man who could also wear tight black pants, boots and a mask and look sexy as hell was hard to come by. But that was a fact Alex would have to learn to live with.

Tomorrow she was going home.

Chapter Ten

"She's almost asleep," Spencer said as he laid Camilla Rose in her crib.

Alex stood beside him and looked down at her niece. Camilla was wearing Winnie the Pooh footed pajamas and was rosy-cheeked from her bath. Although her eyelashes were drooping, she still managed to smile up at Spencer.

"It's okay if Camilla falls asleep during my little talk with the girls," Alex said. "She's crazy about you already." *And who can blame her,* she added to herself as she surreptitiously took a sideways look at the "at-home" Zorro.

Spencer had taken off the mask, hat, cape and boots, but even without those dashing accoutrements, he was one fetching fellow. He'd untucked his black shirttail and rolled up his sleeves to just below the elbows to keep them from getting wet while he bathed Camilla—a sight Alex could never forget even without the help of the pictures she'd taken during the bubble-fest.

He still wore the black pants, too, but was padding around in a pair of white socks. His hair was disheveled and he smelled of baby powder and bubble-bath. In other words, he projected a devastating image that combined both danger and domesticity. What woman wouldn't be intrigued?

But it wasn't a woman Spencer was trying to win over, Alex reminded herself. It was two little girls who would soon be finished brushing their teeth and clamoring for their bedtime story. And it was her job to see what she could do to facilitate that winning-over process. Still in her *señorita* costume, she wished she'd had time to dash next door and change into something more comfortable for reading stories, but she wouldn't have missed the bath scene for anything.

But now, her emotions running high, Alex resolutely turned away from the heartwarming sight of Spencer gently tucking the blanket around Camilla. She'd only known this man for two days, but she very much feared she was falling in love with him! Determined to divert her thoughts, she gestured toward a small sofa in the corner of the room. "So...do you sit there when you read to the girls?"

"Yes." Spencer left the crib, flicked on a floor lamp at one end of the sofa and turned off the overhead lights. "Depending on how sleepy she is, sometimes I hold Camilla in my lap and read, sometimes I put her in the crib and she drifts off before I've finished a paragraph. But I've made a habit of reading to them in here so they're all included."

"It's a cozy setup," Alex said approvingly. "Do Elizabeth and Margaret ever sit in your lap or cuddle up to you when you read?"

"I wish," Spencer said ruefully. "No. They sit on either side of me with usually six inches or so of space between me and them. I have to hold the book low on my knees so they can see. A couple of times Maggie's scooted close, but Lizzie gave her the evil eye and Maggie retreated again.'' He sighed and rubbed the back of his neck. ''But they seem to enjoy our reading times together and pay rapt attention to me—'' he gave another rueful grin ''—as long as I'm reading and not talking.''

''Do you always read from a book, or do you make up stories?''

''I always read from a book, and I've got tons of those.'' He pointed to a basketful of them by the dresser. ''If I made up stories, they'd be forced to make eye contact with me and that might not go over so well. Why? Are you going to make up a story?''

She smiled and shrugged. ''Maybe.''

His eyes narrowed with teasing suspicion. ''What kind of story?''

She chuckled. ''I'm not sure yet. I'm playing this whole thing by ear. But, trust me, I'm on your side.''

His grin relaxed to a tender smile. ''I'm glad you're on my side, Alex Koskov.''

She felt herself glowing from the warmth in Spencer's gaze. She was going to miss that warmth. She was going to miss those eyes....

''All brushed and flossed!'' Irma exclaimed as she ushered Elizabeth and Margaret into the bedroom. ''I see Camilla's already zonked out. Wore the poor little thing out today, and she didn't get a nap, either.''

''Camilla's just a baby, but I'm five years old and not sleepy at all,'' Elizabeth announced as she grabbed one of Alex's hands.

''Me neither!'' Margaret chorused, grabbing

Alex's other hand and pulling her toward the sofa. "We're ready for our story, Alex!"

"Okay, but let's not talk too loudly," Alex said in a hushed voice. "We might wake up Camilla."

"I don't think a cannon would wake up that one," Irma gave as her opinion. "And it'd probably take two cannons to wake me up once my head hits the pillow. I'm bushed." She stood on tiptoes and kissed Spencer on the cheek. "'Night, Spence." She turned to the girls and held out her arms with a smile. "Got a kiss for your gran?"

The girls willingly hurried over to Irma, kissed and hugged her, then just as willingly hurried back to Alex. By the sheer force of their enthusiasm, Alex found herself plopped down on the sofa, then both girls squeezed up against her like a couple of bookends. She looked up and saw Spencer observing them wistfully. She hoped she was able to convey with a look how sorry she was that they didn't snuggle up to him in the same way, and how much she was hoping to change that.

"Probably won't see you till morning, Alex," Gran was saying as she exited the room, tugging on Spencer's sleeve so he'd follow. "The front door will be unlocked and there's always a light on in the hall. You know where your bedroom is. 'Night."

"Good night, Irma," Alex managed to say as the spry old gal disappeared through the door, but the last thing she saw was the continued wistful expression on Spencer's face as he left with his grandmother.

"Whew. I'm glad *he's* gone," Elizabeth said, her face turned up to Alex adoringly. "I was afraid he might stay."

"Would that have been so bad?" Alex asked mildly and with a smile. "You don't seem to mind him when he reads to you."

"*I* like it when he reads to us," Margaret confided. "But Elizabeth says we're going to like you reading to us much better."

Alex made no reply to this statement, asking instead, "What if I didn't read to you? What if I made up a story?"

"I like fairy tales," Elizabeth said. "Do you know the story of Cinderella?"

"Do you know Snow White?" Margaret chimed in.

Alex nodded. "Yes. I know both those stories. And I'll bet you know them just as well as I do. Wouldn't you like to hear something different?"

Margaret nodded eagerly, but Elizabeth got a suspicious look in her eyes that for a fleeting second reminded her forcefully of the look Spencer had had in his eyes just minutes before. "What kind of story? If this is a story about daddies, I don't want to hear it. Bernice tried to tell us daddy stories and Gran tried to tell us daddy stories and we didn't like it, did we, Margaret?"

Margaret's eager nodding continued for a second before she realized she was supposed to be shaking her head from side to side instead of up and down. "No, we didn't like the daddy stories," she finally corrected herself, but Alex suspected that Margaret liked the daddy stories quite as much as she liked her new daddy. But she was loyal to her sister and led by her in every behavior.

Having half-concocted a story about a daddy bear and three cubs he'd adopted and the amazing way they'd become a family, Alex realized she was going to have to come up with an approach to get through to the girls that hadn't already been attempted by Irma and Bernice. But what?

Then it hit her. *Honesty.* It was a characteristic highly prized by the head of the household and would no doubt be drummed into the children as they grew up. Maybe, instead of trying to soft-serve what she wanted to say to them about Spencer, she should just tell them plainly and honestly what she thought. Irma and Bernice had had to tread softly for fear of alienating the girls, but, since she'd be leaving tomorrow, Alex had nothing to lose by taking the straightforward approach.

Taking a deep, steadying breath, Alex began, "Do you know why Gran and Bernice tried to tell you stories about daddies, Elizabeth?"

Elizabeth shrugged and looked sullen. "I don't know."

"I think you do know," Alex suggested gently.

Elizabeth crossed her arms and scooted an inch away. "This is boring. I thought you were going to tell us a story?"

"I promise I will, if you'll first let me talk to you for a minute about Dr. Jones."

"Why do you want to talk about *him?*"

"Because I like him very much and I want to help him get a special present he's wanted for a long time, a present he wants more than anything in the whole world."

Margaret leaned on Alex's leg and peered up into her face, her own face alight with curiosity. "What present does he want? Is it his birthday?"

Alex chuckled. "No, it's not his birthday. But if

he got this present, he'd feel like he was having a hundred birthdays and Christmases all rolled into one.''

Margaret's eyes grew wide. ''Tell us! What does he want?''

Alex looked at Elizabeth. Her bottom lip was out and she was staring at the floor. Things didn't look good, but Alex was already in this up to her eyeballs and had to see it out.

''He wants you, Elizabeth, Camilla Rose and him to be a family.''

Margaret's brow puckered as she said, ''But we already live in the same house.''

''That doesn't make you a family,'' Alex explained. She looked at Elizabeth for a reaction, but she'd turned her face away. Alex forged on. ''Families play together, work together, *talk* to one another. I've noticed that you don't talk to Dr. Jones at all. Why is that?''

Alex waited. Margaret watched her sister anxiously and waited, too. She probably was just as eager for an explanation as Alex was. The seconds that ticked by seemed like hours, but Alex considered it a good sign that Elizabeth hadn't left the room or angrily demanded to know why she wasn't reading them a story as she'd promised.

Alex's patience paid off when Elizabeth said in a very low voice, ''I don't want Dr. Jones to be our daddy.''

''Why not, sweetheart? He's very nice, and I know he's grown to love all three of you girls since you came to live here.''

Elizabeth squeezed her eyes shut and shook her

head. "*No!* I don't want him to adopt us. He *can't* be our daddy!

"Is it because you miss your other daddy?"

"No," Elizabeth choked out. "I *don't* miss my other daddy."

Alex's heart went out to her niece as she watched a tear roll down her cheek. She understand only too well why Elizabeth might not miss Richard, but she also realized how guilty it might make a little girl feel not to have so-called "natural" feelings toward her father.

"It's okay to feel the way you do, Elizabeth," Alex tried to reassure her. "The people we love usually have earned that love. We don't have to love someone just because they're related to us. We try, of course, but sometimes..."

Alex's words trailed off into a sort of helpless shake of her head. She didn't want to get mired in a long, heavy explanation about familial dynamics. And she couldn't very well tell Elizabeth that she understood her feelings toward Richard because she was Richard's sister and didn't miss him, either. Elizabeth wasn't ready for that much honesty, and neither was Alex. She'd wait again and see what Elizabeth came up with on her own.

She was rewarded for her patience when Elizabeth finally turned to look at her. She wasn't crying. The single tear Alex had seen roll down Elizabeth's plump cheek before had probably been involuntary and much fought against.

"Daddies don't read to you," she said solemnly. "Daddies don't tuck you in bed and kiss you goodnight. Daddies go away on long trips. And sometimes they yell at you and mommy...and they *al-*

ways yell at the nannies and send them away just when you've got used to them.''

Ah, so that was it! Now Alex thought she understood why Elizabeth was resisting accepting Spencer as her new daddy. Sure, she'd figured all along that part of the reason was that the girls simply needed time to adjust after losing their parents and after being transplanted from one sort of life to another very different sort of life. And some children would be nervous about getting close to new guardians for fear of losing them, too. But Alex had figured all along that there was more to Elizabeth's reluctance to accept Spencer than that. After all, they'd warmed up to Gran and Bernice and even to her. Why not to Spencer? It certainly couldn't be because he wasn't loving or lovable enough.

The key to it all seemed to be a bit of childish logic gone awry, causing Elizabeth to balk at the idea of the kind Dr. Jones becoming a ''daddy'' as defined by the only other daddy they'd ever known…Richard. It was easy to see why she'd conclude that if Richard's behavior personified what a daddy was, then they'd rather keep Dr. Jones!

After all, Dr. Jones read to them and tucked them in bed. He didn't go away on long trips or yell at them like Richard did. Elizabeth must be worried that if she let Dr. Jones into her heart, that if he became the ''official'' daddy in their lives, he'd suddenly start behaving like Richard!

So, now that she was pretty sure she understood what lay behind Elizabeth's refusal to talk to Spencer and accept him as her new daddy, what exactly did she do about it? It was one thing understanding a problem, it was another thing going about the task of fixing that problem.

Now it was Elizabeth's turn to wait. Margaret's, too. They both looked at Alex expectantly. She was very nervous. She wanted to say the right thing, to come up with just the right words to take away Elizabeth's anxiety and enable her to risk letting Spencer into her life, thereby also releasing her loyal little sister to do the same. But she didn't want to come right out and say Richard had been a bad person or a bad daddy. She knew Spencer would not approve of that.

Alex took Elizabeth's hands in hers. "Elizabeth, I want you to know that all daddies are…well… different."

"What do you mean?"

"Every daddy is a *person,* too. A person who has certain personality traits."

Elizabeth cocked her head to the side. "Personality traits?"

"That just means the way a person acts and thinks. And the way a person acts and thinks before he or she becomes a mommy or a daddy generally carries over into the kind of parent they become. For example, if a person yelled a lot *before* he became a daddy, chances are he'd still be yelling a lot *after* he became a daddy. Sometimes even yelling at the people he loves, like his wife and his children. Do you know what I mean?"

Elizabeth's brow puckered. "I *think* so."

"Good, because, you see, Dr. Jones is a nice person. He's always been a nice person. He's the type of person who will always tell you stories and tuck you into bed, and try very hard never to yell at you, whether he's your daddy or not. Do you understand what I'm trying to tell you, Elizabeth?''

She nodded uncertainly. ''You're saying that if Dr. Jones was our daddy, he would still read to us and tuck us in bed and he wouldn't yell at us like our other daddy did?''

''Honey, I can pretty much guarantee it. In fact, if you talked to Dr. Jones and actually treated him like the daddy he wants to be to you, nothing in the world could stop him from doing those things…not even if someone offered him a zillion dollars!''

Margaret giggled. ''A *zillion* dollars?''

Elizabeth smiled, but still looked a little dubious. ''Does your daddy yell at you, Alex?''

Alex laughed. ''Not at me, sweetie. But he does yell at other people when he gets upset. He's even been known to pound his fist on tables to get his point across. But underneath all that gruffness is a man made of marshmallows.''

The idea and the corresponding mental image of a man made out of marshmallows set Margaret to giggling again, and Elizabeth even chuckled.

''But you have to remember, Elizabeth, that no one is perfect. Even really nice people raise their voices now and then when they get very upset. I know I have a few times. And I'll bet even you have once or twice.''

''She's yelled at me,'' Margaret supplied helpfully.

Elizabeth scowled her sister down and Alex continued. ''Well, you see what I mean, then. But Elizabeth doesn't usually yell at you, does she, Margaret?''

Margaret shook her head. ''No.''

"That's because she's not a yeller. And Dr. Jones is no yeller, either. He's not the type to want to yell at anyone, and he especially doesn't want to yell at you girls. He loves you too much."

Elizabeth nodded thoughtfully and Alex remained silent for a minute or two while everything she'd said hopefully sank in. Then she pulled both girls into a hug and said, "What about that story now? I'll tell you Snow White and Cinderella if you want. Or how about another fairy tale, like the one my mother used to tell me…Rapunzel? Or there's always Sleeping Beauty? You can choose."

The girls argued companionably for a minute, then decided on Rapunzel. Alex remembered the story well from her mother's repeated telling of the fairy tale when she was a little girl, and she gave it all the theatrical voices and facial expressions her mother employed to entertain her daughter and send her to bed full of happy and fanciful images. The girls listened with avid interest and when the story was over naturally begged for another. Alex agreed to a short story from one of their books, but first extracted a promise from them to go to bed right afterward without fussing.

The girls were as good as their word, probably owing in part to being very tired and sleepy after their long, exciting day, and they went straight to the bedroom they shared, which was right next door to Camilla's. They scrambled into their beds and Alex had them tucked in, kissed good-night and was almost to the door when Elizabeth asked in a small, shy voice, "Isn't Dr. Jones going to tuck us in, too?"

Although she was still calling him Dr. Jones, Alex

considered Elizabeth's reminder to be a very good sign. She smiled approvingly and said, "I'm sure he would like to. I'll go get him."

As Alex went down the stairs, she met Spencer coming up. She returned his inquisitive and hopeful gaze with a neutral expression and a subdued smile. She didn't want to get his hopes up *too* high about what she might have accomplished with the girls. "Elizabeth and Margaret are waiting for you to tuck them in."

"I thought I heard you guys vacating the nursery," he said, then asked eagerly, "How'd it go?"

"It's too soon to tell. But I think I understand what's been at the root of the problem. I'll wait downstairs for you and we'll talk after you've tucked the girls in."

He nodded, searched her face another moment as if looking for clues, then said, "I've made a fire in the library," before continuing up the stairs to the girls' bedroom.

Alex went to the library where a cheerful fire was indeed burning brightly, lending a warm, mellow glow to the entire large room where only a single lamp was turned on over the desk. She walked around, examining the pictures on the walls, the books on the shelves, the knickknacks and such that revealed a man's habits and hobbies.

Apparently he liked the classics but enjoyed many of the recent bestsellers, too. It appeared that he liked to golf and fish. And judging by a small TV tucked in the corner and a video collection of Abbot and Costello movies, the Three Stooges and Bob Hope, he liked a good, old-fashioned belly laugh, too. Copies of *Casablanca* and *An Affair to Remem-*

ber proved he was romantic, unless of course they were movies of Irma's that she'd brought over to watch when she was baby-sitting.

A man's favorite room told a great deal about him, Alex mused. Especially when it came to the photos he kept on the mantel. Spencer's fireplace had a deep mantel and it was covered with family pictures that went back three or four generations. She could easily guess by the clothes, hairstyles and family resemblances, just who was who.

There were his father and mother, his grandmother and grandfather. There was an early family photo of him with his parents and siblings. She discovered that he had two older sisters and that he'd been darn cute as a kid, too! There was a picture that had at least fifty people in it, no doubt a Jones family reunion. Family was obviously very important to Spencer, and in the midst of all these family photos, resting smack-dab in the honored center of them, were photos of Elizabeth, Margaret and Camilla Rose.

Gazing at the pictures of her nieces, Alex knew with a certainty that she'd made the right decision to support the adoption of the girls into the Jones family fold. Blood ties be damned, this was where they belonged. She just hoped her father would someday be admitted into the circle of people who were fortunate enough to be a part of the girls' lives. She figured it was really up to her dad. If he just backed off the custody suit and talked rationally with Spencer, she was sure Spencer was fair-minded enough to work something out with him.

"Would you like a drink, or some hot chocolate or something?"

Alex twirled around, her hand on her throat. "My goodness, you creep up on a person like a cat!"

He grinned. "It's my training as a masked hero. I'm used to sneaking around."

Her gaze flickered over him as he stood just inside the library door. His hair was still mussed, the firelight picking out bright strands of silver-gold. The sight of his black shirt with the tail out and the black pants that made him look even more slim-hipped than usual still played havoc with her heartbeat. Sexily disheveled was the best way to describe him. That…and dangerous. It was a darn good thing she was leaving in the morning. But that meant tonight was goodbye. A sadness crept over her like a shroud of fog.

"By the look on your face, I'm afraid you've got bad news for me." He walked toward her, concern etching lines on either side of his beautiful mouth.

She forced herself to quit thinking about how attractive and wonderful Spencer was and how much she was going to miss him. Right now probably the only thing on his mind—the only thing that should be on *her* mind, too—was how things had gone with the girls.

She smiled. "No, the news isn't bad. But it isn't necessarily good, either. I feel like I might have got through to Elizabeth, but you probably won't know for a day or two. How'd the tucking-in go?"

He shrugged. "I tucked the blankets around them, kissed them on the forehead and said, 'good-night, sleep tight,' like I always do. They looked at me solemnly without saying a word, then turned over on their sides and closed their eyes…like they always do. Although I do think Elizabeth looked at me a little differently tonight…. Is that possible, Alex?'' he ended hopefully.

Her smile broadened. ''It's possible.''

He sat down on one end of the leather sofa that faced the fire, invited her to sit down, too, then gave her his earnest attention while she told him basically what had transpired during her talk with the girls. When she finished, he sat and gazed into the fire for several minutes.

Alex was content to wait and watch Spencer's thoughtful profile till he was ready to speak. And it was during that quiet interlude that she finally admitted to herself that she was not just in danger of falling in love with Spencer…she already had. Crazy and ironic as it seemed, she'd fallen in love for the first time in her life with a man she'd only known two days. A man, moreover, whom she had no business being in love with at all.

That's when she decided that she could no longer sit with him, talk with him, be with him, under false pretenses. And she wasn't going to skulk out of town, as she'd originally intended, leaving him to find out who she really was at a later date.

She rallied her courage and was just about to interrupt his reflections, when he turned and smiled at her. It was a smile tender enough to melt the heart of Atilla the Hun. Needless to say, for a woman desperately in love with the man behind the smile, Alex's heart didn't have a prayer.

''Thank you, Alex,'' he said. ''Thank you for helping me with the girls. Even if your little talk doesn't make them change toward me overnight, I think it will help in the long run. You handled it just the way I would handle it if only they'd talk to me. With honesty." He took her hand in his and rubbed it warmly. "I'll always be grateful to you."

This was too much for Alex. She snatched her hand away and rose swiftly to her feet, then began to pace the rug in front of the fireplace. "I'm the last person you should feel gratitude toward, Spencer. If I helped you in some small way with the girls, it was the least I could do after presuming on your trust the way I have."

"What?"

When she finally stopped pacing and dared to look at him, Alex saw that Spencer's expression was puzzled, surprised. Despite standing in front of the fire, she suddenly felt cold and crossed her arms tightly over her chest. She shook her head and laughed shakily. "I haven't been honest with you, Spencer," she confessed. "I've been lying to you ever since I first stepped foot in Jonesville."

He stared at her, his brows drawn together. "What are you talking about, Alex?"

She shook her head again and resumed pacing. "You're a good, decent man, Spencer Jones, and honesty is high on your list of values. Although I want you to understand that I'm not usually such a sneak and a liar, I thought I had good reason to lower my own standards and resort to whatever means necessary to accomplish what I set out to do."

He stood up and walked to her, grasping her upper arms and forcing her to stand still. He peered into her face, concern radiating from his eyes. "I don't know what you're talking about, Alex, but I can see you're very upset." He rubbed her arms. "My God, you're shaking like a leaf!"

"Oh, please don't be nice to me," she pleaded, tears welling in her eyes. "If you only knew—"

"Is this about Dimitri? Has he—?"

She stamped her foot. "No! This isn't about Dimitri! There *is* no Dimitri! I made him up, Spencer. I made him up so you wouldn't feel uncomfortable if I hung around with you and the girls. I made him up so—"

"You made him up? There is no Dimitri?" He seemed stunned. His hands gripped her shoulders tightly.

"No. Like I said, I made him—"

"You're not engaged?"

"Spencer, if you want to know the truth, the whole ugly truth, you have to quit interrupting me," she exclaimed, frustrated. "No, I'm not engaged. And I even faked a cough when I came to your office the other day, because I needed an excuse to see you, talk to you. But that's just the tip of the ice—"

But she didn't get the second syllable out. In fact, she was unable to utter another word, because Spencer pulled her hard against his chest, lowered his head, then covered her mouth with his.

Alex knew she should resist. She knew she shouldn't be enjoying the embrace of a man who had no idea how deceitful she'd been and what she'd intended against his family. But the exciting feel of his lips, his warm, seeking tongue, his hands caressing her face, her neck, her back, was as wrenchingly emotional as it was explosively physical.

She loved him. She wanted him to make love to her right there in the library in front of the fire. But—

He drew back for a minute, leaving her feeling bereft. She opened her eyes and he smiled down at her. "You're still trembling. Would I be an egotist if I said I hoped you were trembling because I just kissed you?"

"I think you know what you do to me, Spencer," she whispered brokenly.

He groaned and pulled her close again, his cheek resting against hers. "I feel the same way about you, Alex. I think you know that, too."

Now, Alex, she told herself. *Now is the time to stop this. To stop this and tell the truth.* But it was hard to let go of heaven when you had it in your arms....

Her eyes fluttered shut again as he kissed her neck lingeringly, moving from her ear to the pounding pulse at the base of her throat. His hands wended their way up her back, then around to the front. He cupped her aching breasts, flooding her entire body with warmth and desire. When he teased the hard nipples between his thumb and forefinger, she wanted to die from the sheer pleasure of it.

"No, Spencer," she managed to rasp.

He immediately drew back and looked down at her. "I'm sorry, Alex. Am I going too fast? Is it because the girls are upstairs? I hope you're not worried about Bernice, because while she's a wonderful person and I plan to have a long, honest talk with her to clear things up between us, we could never—"

"It's not Bernice. It's me. I can't—"

"Look, I know you've got a great job and you probably don't want some small-town guy with three little girls tying you down, but we could work something out. In case you're wondering, this isn't just a physical thing with me. I care about you.''

"But you don't know anything about me, Spencer,'' Alex said with a sad shake of her head.

He smiled indulgently. "If you've got a checkered past, sweetheart, I think I can—''

But what he thought he could do would have to wait. Just then the doorbell rang. With one arm still around her waist, Spencer frowned and looked at his watch. "Wonder who that could be?''

Alex didn't care who it was. She was just grateful they'd interrupted what could have amounted to the biggest mistake of her life. Oh, she'd have enjoyed a mistake that involved making love with Spencer Jones, all right. But the pleasure and the memory of it would be bittersweet, tainted with the realization of her dishonesty and the look on Spencer's face when she told him the truth afterward.

Whoever was at the door apparently wasn't a particularly patient person. Now they were knocking on the door insistently.

"Don't move. I'll be right back,'' Spencer told her as he slowly released her and walked backward toward the hall. He shook his head, grinning. "Did I tell you how delectable you look in that dress?''

She chuckled weakly, but her smile fell away the minute he disappeared down the hall. She turned toward the fire again, grimly awaiting his return. She was determined that she wouldn't let him take her in his arms again and distract her so completely from what she needed to say and do.

There was a murmur of deep voices from the hall, then two sets of rapid footsteps coming toward the library. Self-consciously aware that she was still wearing her *señorita* costume and the flushed look of a woman who'd just been kissed, she waited nervously for this unexpected visitor.

As he stepped into the room, Alex's blood froze in her veins. It was her father.

Chapter Eleven

Alex wished the floor would just open up and swallow her. Here were the two men she loved more than anything or anyone else in the world, and both of them were looking at her as if she'd just plunged daggers into their hearts! But she supposed that's exactly what betrayal felt like.

"Dad...! How did you know where I was?"

"So he *is* your father? You're that...that *creep,* Richard Ethington's, sister?"

"Don't call him a creep," her father snarled.

"I'm his half sister," Alex admitted in a small voice.

Spencer shook his head disbelievingly. "When Mr. Big Shot Millionaire here demanded to see his daughter, I didn't have a clue what he was talking about. I figured he'd just come up with some kind of cockamamy story to get into the house to see the girls. But then he said he saw your car parked out front, the car he'd just bought for you four days ago. Then he said your name...*Alexandra.* I only knew of one female named Alexandra passing through Jonesville." He shook his head again. "What kind of game are you playing, Alex?"

"That's what I'd like to know, Lex," her father said angrily but with an undercurrent of hurt in his voice. "When you called earlier today, I knew something was up. It took me a while, but then I finally figured out that you were probably here. Damned if I know why, but it appears you've switched sides on me! I can't believe you'd be so naive as to fall for this guy's Romeo tactics! He's just using you, Lex, can't you see that?"

"*Me* using *her?*" Spencer exclaimed. "She's the one that came to my office pretending to have a sore throat. She's the one who finagled her way into my grandmother's house, then just as adroitly slipped in here. She cozied up to me, then she cozied up to the girls and was up there with them tonight, all alone—and with my blessing!—telling them God only knows what!" Spencer rubbed his jaw distractedly. "What a fool I've been!"

Alex's throat felt painfully constricted. "Spencer, you don't understand—"

"What's not to understand? You said it yourself just ten minutes ago. You've been lying to me ever since you set foot in Jonesville. But I thought you'd only lied about Dimitri and faking your sore throat."

"Who the hell's Dimitri?" her father demanded.

Ignoring the interruption, Spencer continued bitterly. "But I only have myself to blame. I was ready and willing to forgive you for making up a cough and a phony fiancé because I was flattered to have a woman like you go to such lengths just to be with me. But all along, what you really wanted was to get to the girls, prejudice them against me and see what you could find out or fabricate to help along your father's custody suit."

By now Alex was barely able to hold back the sob that was gathering in the back of her throat. If she spoke, she'd cry, so she said nothing.

Spencer stared at her, his eyes full of pain. "You can't deny any of it, can you? You've been using me and plotting to destroy my family."

Put that way, what she'd originally set out to do when she came to Jonesville did seem downright cruel. She wouldn't blame him if he hated her. But a part of her wanted him to see her side of the story, to make him understand the motivation behind her actions.

She swallowed the huge ache in her throat and forced back the threatening tears. "I was going to tell you. I was *trying* to tell you when my father came to the door. I was going to explain it all, confess all the lies, but you...but you wouldn't let me finish. You kept kissing me and I couldn't even—"

"He was kissing you. *Hmph.*" Her father made a disgusted face. "Is it any wonder I'm suspicious about your sudden change of heart, Lex? You agreed that those girls belonged with me...with their real family. Then you call me on the phone and say you're not so sure anymore." He jabbed a finger in Spencer's direction. "This small-town sawbones put you up to it, didn't he?"

"Cut the crap, Ethington," Spencer said, his voice contemptuous. "I didn't put her up to anything. But can you say the same? Maybe you put her up to spying on me. Maybe you're as good an actor as she is and you're not really surprised or dismayed to find her here at all. Although I'm not sure what you thought you'd gain by showing up like this, if you don't leave immediately, I'm calling the police.''

"Call the police," her father shouted. "I'll force a fight and we'll end up in matching jail cells for disturbing the peace. But with my lawyers, I'll be out of there in the blink of an eye.''

"Maybe not. You'll face an additional charge for trespassing.''

"Like hell. You invited me in!''

"Stop it, both of you," Alex begged. "You sound like children! Have you forgotten that there're some real children trying to sleep upstairs? I just hope they haven't heard any of this!''

Both men looked shame-faced, but Spencer couldn't resist getting in a last jab. "Like you really care about the girls, Alex. Even that was an act, wasn't it?''

"She cares about the girls," her father said, instinctively coming to her defense. "She just knew they'd be better off with me, that's all.'' He looked confused, then mumbled, "Or she used to. Hell, I don't know *which* side she's on anymore!''

"There shouldn't be two sides," Alex said, the tears she'd been repressing finally slipping down her face. "There should be only one side…whatever's best for the girls. Surely the two of you can sit down and come to an understanding without dragging this through the courts.''

"It's too late for that," Spencer stated, his expression stony. "Before you sued for custody, Ethington—'' he turned accusing eyes toward Alex. "—and before you sent your daughter as a spy to my home, I would have agreed to allow you visiting privileges with the girls. You could have been as much a part of the girls' lives as you wanted, but you forced me to fight back.''

''Why should I have to be allowed rights to my own flesh and blood?'' her father blustered. ''You have no real rights to those children. You are *nothing* to those children—''

''You're wrong, Ethington. I'm their father,'' Spencer returned with steely emphasis.

''Richard was their father!''

''Maybe he was, but he's not anymore. And he was a hell of a bad father from what I've gathered.''

''He was their flesh and blood, just like *I'm* their flesh and blood. You're nobody, Jones. Nobody.''

Something glittered in Spencer's eyes and, despite the commendable control he'd shown so far over his temper, Alex had a horrible feeling that her highly agitated father had just heaped the last straw on the camel's back. She instinctively stepped between the two men, placing a hand on each of their chests as if she could somehow keep them separated if they came to blows.

Spencer, with surprising gentleness, pushed her aside. ''Don't worry,'' he said without looking at her. ''I'm not going to hit your father and, once he hears what I've got to say, he's not going to hit me, either.''

''What the hell are you talking about now, Jones?'' her father returned irritably. ''What could you possibly say that would make me feel different about this damnable situation?''

Spencer crossed his arms and seemed to visibly relax. Even the harsh, angry line of his lips tilted up a little in a smile, as if he were finally unburdening himself of some tremendous secret. Could this be about Karlie's letter?

"Karlie wanted me to keep this to myself for as long as possible, but the time has come, Ethington, to tell you—"

Gruffly he asked, "Tell me what?"

"That Margaret and Camilla Rose are, indeed, your flesh and blood...a phrase you seem terribly fond of. But Elizabeth isn't. Elizabeth is *my* flesh and blood. Lizzie is my daughter."

At first Alex and her father were too stunned to do anything but stare at Spencer. He stared defiantly back, then abruptly turned away and walked to the fireplace where he stood with his back to them, his hand on the mantelpiece, his head bent and his gaze apparently fixed on the flames of the fire. Eventually Alex and her father stirred, exchanged startled and perturbed glances, then moved to hover uncertainly a few feet behind Spencer.

"What did you say, Jones?" her father demanded to know in the quietest voice he'd used since entering the house, a voice that was tremulous with shock.

Spencer did not immediately reply. Finally he turned and looked first at Alex, then at her father. He appeared both weary and wary.

"It was my ace," he said. "I was holding it until you absolutely forced me to play it, but I was pretty sure that would never happen. I figured it would take a lot of time and involve a lot of hassles, but as long as I could protect the girls from being affected by it, I was willing to endure a long court battle to keep them. I figured the odds were in my favor that I'd win in the end. But, if things got sticky, if you didn't play fair, I knew I had the take-it-all hand.''

"Your ace," her father repeated dully. "You mean Elizabeth.''

"Yes. Elizabeth. Lizzie is my natural daughter.''

It hardly seemed necessary to say it out loud, but Alex's lips moved without conscious will. "Karlie was pregnant when she married Richard.''

Spencer nodded. "Yes, she was.''

"Did Richard know?'' her father asked.

"Yes. They decided together to say the baby was his. Karlie indicated in the letter that while Richard was prepared to marry a woman pregnant with another man's baby, he wasn't prepared for the whole world to know the truth. Karlie was barely a month along when they married, and Lizzie was so obliging as to come three weeks late, which gave credence to the lie. They told everyone she was a week early, a baby conceived on their honeymoon.''

His smile was bitter and brittle as he added, "So, you see, Ethington, Karlie and your son have been raising *my* flesh and blood all this time. Kind of a raw deal, don't you think?''

"How could Karlie do that to you?'' Alex whispered.

Spencer said nothing, but his eyes seemed to mock her. He was probably thinking, *How could you do what you did?*

"But why would my son leave his other daughters to you, Jones?'' her father asked. "They aren't yours, too, are they?''

Spencer gave him a beleaguered look before answering. "Of course not. I haven't set eyes on Karlie since the night before our scheduled wedding. I suspect Karlie was completely faithful to her husband, which is more than I can say for Richard. Karlie got Richard to agree to granting me guardianship of the girls in exchange for staying with him despite his numerous affairs. He didn't relish a messy divorce, and I think he must have loved her in his way and wanted to keep her...in his way.''

He shrugged. ''Besides, what were the chances of both of them dying together like they did? I don't suppose Richard thought guardianship of the girls would ever become an issue. He probably felt pretty smug about appeasing Karlie by signing a joint will that would never be needed.''

A muscle worked in his jaw. ''If Karlie and Richard hadn't died so tragically, I might have gone my whole life without ever knowing I had a daughter. Not a particularly fair conclusion either way.''

Alex was still puzzled about something. ''But, even now, even after they're gone and buried, Karlie didn't want you to tell anyone that Elizabeth is your daughter?''

''She wanted to keep the girls together and she thought there'd be a better chance of that if no one but me knew Elizabeth was mine. She asked me not to seek custody of Elizabeth alone. She trusted me to honor her wishes.'' He looked pointedly at her father. ''She wasn't sure what anyone else would do, or how they might use that information. A judge might have given Elizabeth to me and the other girls to your father, dividing them...which was the last thing Karlie wanted to happen.''

''So why are you telling me this now?'' her father asked. ''What makes you think I won't use the information just as Karlie was afraid I might? What if

I sue for custody of Margaret and Camilla Rose and argue to the judge that you're getting your natural daughter, so why shouldn't I get *my* natural grand-daughters?''

"Dad, you wouldn't do that, would you?'' Alex exclaimed, dismayed. ''The girls belong together!''

"I told you because I'm depending on you to do the right thing, Ethington. Karlie wasn't sure what you'd do, but, although you're a pompous windbag, I'm willing to concede that you might have a heart beating under that French-tailored shirt you're wear-ing and really do—in your strange way—have the girls' best interests at heart.''

Her father's chest swelled up a little and his face got redder, but Alex was relieved that he allowed Spencer to finish making his point.

"You know now there's no way you'll ever get Elizabeth, and that if you somehow managed to get the judge to overturn the will signed by both your son and your daughter-in-law and were granted guardianship of Margaret and Camilla Rose, you'd be separating them from their sister. You and I both know that would devastate them.''

There was a pause before her father answered, almost wistfully, ''I've always wanted what was best for them. And I've always felt strongly that I could provide them with everything they need.''

"But you haven't seen them since they were small, and Camilla Rose you've never seen at all.''

"That's not my—''

"I never said it was your fault. I don't know the particulars, but I can readily believe your son might have made it impossible for you to be an active grandfather to the girls. But these are the facts—the girls are settled here. They are loved and cared for by me and my grandmother, and will someday have a full-time mother.''

Alex felt her heart flutter painfully and her cheeks burn with shame and chagrin. The girls would indeed have a mother someday...and Spencer a wife. But it wouldn't be her. Never her.

''They're still adjusting to their new family, but I have no doubt that eventually they *will* adjust.'' Spencer turned to look at Alex, his expression guarded and remote. ''I just hope they haven't suffered a setback tonight.''

Alex knew he referred to her bedtime talk with the girls. He obviously still distrusted her and wasn't sure, despite how she'd tried to explain herself, that she hadn't worsened his situation with the girls by saying mean and untruthful things about him. It made her sick with sadness to realize he probably wouldn't even believe her if she attempted to reassure him now, but she had to try.

''Spencer, I may have initially misrepresented myself to you—''

He raised a brow.

''Okay, I've lied to you. But I wasn't lying when I said I wanted to help you with the girls. I did, as my father accused me, switch sides...for want of a better term. Everything I told you in the library about my conversation with the girls was the God's truth. Please believe me.''

While Spencer's blue eyes sharply and suspiciously studied her, Alex remembered how he used to look at her. How he'd been looking at her just a few minutes before. With warmth, tenderness, desire…and love? It was keen misery to realize he'd never look at her like that again.

Spencer wanted to believe her, but did he dare? She hadn't been honest with him from the start. But she claimed she'd changed her mind about her position on where the girls belonged and seemed to regret the things she'd done. Hadn't she been about to make a full confession earlier? Or had she just been playing another angle?

Hell, he didn't know! His brain was a muddle and he was so damned disappointed and disillusioned he didn't know what to believe. Before her father showed up, he'd been well on his way to falling in love with Alexandra Koskov. Even now, as he stared into her beautiful gray-green eyes—eyes shiny with tears—he wasn't sure if he hadn't already fallen in love with her.

"I think it's time to go, Lex." Ethington had taken hold of his daughter's arm and was gently tugging. Alexandra seemed reluctant to break eye contact with him, but finally turned away and walked slowly with her father toward the door.

"What are you going to do?" Spencer asked.

Alexandra turned expectantly around, forcing Spencer to clarify his question. "Ethington…. What are you going to do about the girls?" Alex looked embarrassed and turned again to face the door.

"I don't know," Ethington answered grimly.

Spencer sighed. He chastised himself for indulging in a tiny hope that Ethington would make a quick turnabout. He was a proud man who might not be ready to concede defeat. But Spencer was not without compassion for him. He probably did truly want the girls for the right reasons, but he had certainly mishandled things in his attempts to win custody. The idea of sending Alex in to spy on him...! Well, *if* that's what he'd done... But that was something else Spencer wasn't sure about.

The bottom line was, he and Ethington could have worked things out. He had been sincere about including the girls' grandfather in their lives. But now he wasn't so sure.

They'd reached the library door, Ethington opened it and he and Alexandra were about to pass through when she turned. Her cheeks were still damp with tears, but she raised her head proudly and jutted out that beautiful chin of hers.

"I just want you to know, Spencer, that my father had no idea I was here. He had no part in this plot to spy on you. It was all my doing, and I'm...I'm very sorry. I'm sorry I lied to you and I'm sorry I messed things up with Bernice. But I'm sure you can fix them...if you want to."

Without waiting for a reply, she turned and they crossed the hall and quickly exited through the front door.

For several minutes, Spencer simply stood where he was, his mind and heart reeling from the events of that day, particularly the last half hour. He still wasn't sure what or who to believe. He didn't know if he was crazy to hope Ethington would drop the custody suit or not. He had no idea what the future held in respect to the girls and his continued desire to make them a bona fide family...both legally and through the even stronger ties of the heart.

But one thing he did know for sure. He wasn't going to "fix" things with Bernice. While he hoped to be her good friend always, he knew he could never marry her. Why would Alex think that what happened here tonight would change his feelings toward Bernice? What he'd told her about wanting a woman he could love heart and soul—not just a good mother for the girls—was the truth. Falling in love with Alex had made the idea of settling for anything less intolerable.

Kneading the back of his neck, he moved with weary steps to the stairs and up to bed, flipping off lights as he went. He might be depressed as hell tonight, but tomorrow three little girls still needed him to be "Daddy."

ALEX ENTERED IRMA'S HOUSE as quietly as possible, gathered her belongings and left without waking her hostess. She thought about leaving a note, but what would she say?

Fortunately she and her father had to drive separate cars to the Lancaster airport, so conversation was impossible. She wasn't sure what to say to him, either. She just hoped she hadn't alienated him forever by "switching sides" and supporting Spencer's guardianship of the girls. She and her dad had always been able to talk, but nothing this serious had ever come between them before.

And the shock of finding out Elizabeth was Spencer's daughter...! By the equal way he treated the girls, by the equal love he showed for all three, you'd never know that only Elizabeth was his biological child. Alex was more and more impressed with Spencer Jones...and more and more hopelessly in love.

Yeah, *hopeless* was certainly the right word in this case. Even if her father and Spencer eventually came to an understanding over the girls and her father became part of their lives, she'd probably never be welcomed into the fold. Even if Spencer *did* forgive her and allowed her access to the girls, she wouldn't be able to bear being near him, only to be reminded of what she could never have.

At the airport, her father left his rented car with an airport employee and made arrangements for her car to be driven back to Boston the next day. With his money he could arrange just about anything. They boarded his private jet, and once the plane reached cruising altitude and the flight attendant had served her father with brandy and her with decaf, they were left alone.

Alex sipped on her coffee, both dreading and desiring the moment her father would speak.

"I'm not one for putting things off," he began finally. "And even though we're both tired and dispirited, Lex, I think we'd better hash this business out now."

"Mom always did say never let the sun go down on your anger," Alex said wistfully.

Her father sighed and smiled sadly. "I'm not angry, hon. I was, but I'm not now."

Alex set down her cup and threw her arms around her father's neck, her eyes welling with tears again. "Oh, Dad! I'm so relieved. I couldn't stand it if you stayed mad at me."

Her father rubbed her back. "Don't you think I've learned anything from my experiences with Richard? I'll never stay mad at you, no matter what you do."

She drew back and peered up at him questioningly. "But you might still disapprove of what I do or disagree with me, right? I've got to know, Dad. Do you still think I betrayed you, or do you understand why I changed my mind and decided to support Spencer's guardianship of the girls?''

He frowned. "I'm not sure how I feel about the whole mess just yet. I'm still shocked to learn that Elizabeth isn't even related to me! She still *feels* like my granddaughter."

"Oh, Dad, you don't have to have blood ties to someone to feel that kind of love and kinship."

"I guess not. Apparently Jones doesn't," he mused. "But it sure puts a different spin on this dilemma, and certainly makes me understand Jones's behavior better."

She sat back in her seat. "How do you mean?"

"He was reluctant to take the girls at first, but Karlie's letter changed his mind. Now we know why. But I must say I'm surprised that he didn't ignore her request to take all three girls when he could have just taken Elizabeth. After Karlie ran out on him like she did, then kept her pregnancy a secret and raised his daughter as an Ethington, you'd think he'd harbor some hard feelings for her."

"Well, if he did harbor hard feelings for Karlie, Spencer's the type of man who wouldn't let that stand in the way of doing the right thing." She chewed her lip, then suggested, "Maybe he's forgiven her?"

"And maybe he'll forgive you, is that what you're thinking?" her father asked gruffly.

She sighed. "Am I so transparent?"

"It's as plain as the nose on my face that you're hung up on the guy." He looked at her worriedly. "How is that possible so quickly? Can you blame me for thinking he was trying to pull the wool over your eyes by romancing you?''

"But, Dad, why would he do that? He didn't even know who I was till you showed up. Besides, he was right when he told you that I was the one that came on to him. I was trying to get close to him in order to get close to the girls.''

"But it backfired on you, eh?''

"In a big way. I'm stuck on him, but now he thinks I'm the worst kind of sneak.''

Her father patted her hand. "And you did it all for me. You cooked up this plot and were going to see it through without any of my help.''

She gave a rueful smile. "No offense, but what kind of help would you have been? The minute you and Spencer get in the same room, you immediately start shouting. It's too bad he's never seen you in your rational mode.''

Her father shook his head. "I know, hon. But I can't seem to help myself. This thing with the girls has been tearing me up for months. And I still don't know what to do.''

She grasped his hand and looked at him imploringly. "You aren't going to try to take Margaret and Camilla Rose, are you, Dad? Elizabeth and Margaret are so close…you should see them together! And Camilla adores Spencer. He's a wonderful father, too. He reads to them and tucks them into bed.''

"You don't need to sing his praises,'' her father groused. "I know what you think of him…and you're probably right.'' He stared grimly at their joined hands for a moment, then further conceded, "Of course I could never separate the girls. And somehow Jones knew I wouldn't…damn 'im.''

Alex impulsively leaned over and kissed his cheek. "You old softy! I knew you'd do the right thing. And I love you even more!"

"Yeah, well, doing the 'right thing' is all fine and dandy, but while the girls and this paragon, Spencer Jones, might end up happy as clams, where does that leave me? I still want to be a grandfather, and I mean to all three of those girls! Is Jones enough of a nice guy to let that happen?"

"I don't know, Daddy," Alex admitted seriously. "But I think you should give it a try." Her brow smoothed and she smiled, adding, "I think it would help if you talked with the man rather than shouted at him."

Her father chuckled despite himself. "Think so? Well, we'll see. We'll see."

Happy that there was at least hope for her father to reconcile with Spencer and reach an understanding that would enable him to be a grandfather to the girls, Alex leaned her head against his shoulder and closed her eyes, a smile on her lips.

But as images of Spencer floated through her mind, the smile slipped away and her heart ached. Just like Karlie, she'd hurt and disillusioned him. If only she could believe that he'd forgive her as well as her father.

What was that saying, "Once bitten, twice shy?" Well, Spencer had been bitten twice...hard. Did that mean he was *thrice* shy? Any way you looked at it, Spencer couldn't be too eager to put his trust and his heart on the line again.

Chapter Twelve

He was on an airport runway, walking hand in hand with Alexandra through thick fog toward a plane— a small, old-fashioned passenger plane with propellers. They were going on a honeymoon to Spain. He was dressed as Zorro—with the addition of a trenchcoat—and she was the beautiful señorita who had won his heart. She was carrying a small plush toy, a duck that quacked when you squeezed it. She dropped it, and let go of his hand to pick it up.

As she stooped, she disappeared into a swirl of fog. At first he wasn't that worried. He called out her name, but she didn't answer. The fog deepened and thickened. He became frantic and ran through the fog looking for her with the deafening sound of phantom planes roaring in his ears and drowning out his screams.

He kept calling her name.

Alexandra! Alexandra!

A hole appeared in the fog and he could see a plane taking off. It was the plane he and Alexandra were supposed to be on! The plane to Spain. But, wait… Alexandra was on the plane! He could see her smiling face in one of the portals. As the fog

moved in to engulf him again, he watched the plane
disappear into the night sky.

Spencer woke up to a bright, sunlit room...in a
cold sweat.

He sat up and shook his head ruefully. He'd apparently seen *Casablanca* one too many times. The
dream was nonsensical and ridiculous. It made no
sense. But he still couldn't shake that awful feeling
of dread and loss he'd felt when he couldn't find
Alexandra, then saw her leaving on the plane without him.

Determined to dispel the dream and the feelings
it had engendered, Spencer tossed off his blankets
and swung his legs over the side of the bed. That's
when he glanced at his alarm clock for the first time
and was shocked to realize that he'd slept till nine
o'clock.

"Good grief. The girls!"

They, and consequently he, were never in bed
past eight o'clock...and that was even on the week-
ends when they slept in. Gran didn't come over on
Sunday morning as a rule, so he knew she wasn't
watching them. He threw on his robe over the pa-
jama bottoms he'd slept in and quickly headed down
the hall toward the girls' rooms. He wondered why
he didn't hear quacks, or any other happy or dis-
gruntled noises, coming from Camilla's crib.

He went into Camilla's room first and instantly
saw that her crib was empty. Hurrying next door to
Lizzie and Maggie's shared bedroom, he found it
empty as well. He'd checked on them before going
to bed last night and they'd been snug as bugs, not
appearing as though they'd heard a bit of the com-

motion that had gone on downstairs. But where were they now?

Telling himself not to panic, he panicked anyway, running down the stairs to check the rest of the house. He was trying to ignore a crazy notion that had leaped into his brain uninvited…that they had been kidnapped by Ethington and his beautiful, treacherous daughter.

He passed through the hall and went directly to the kitchen, pushing open the swinging door and lunging into the room like a cop on a drug raid. When Lizzie and Maggie looked up from their cereal bowls, and Camilla from her high chair tray dotted with Cheerios, their eyes wide and questioning, he felt like a total idiot. They were seated around the table, as casual as you please, and had even retrieved the newspaper from the front porch and had the comic strip section spread out in front of them.

"Oh. Hi, girls."

As usual, there was no reply to his greeting except from Camilla who happily squealed, then gurgled "Dad-dee" from around a mouthful of Cheerios. Pretending nonchalance now that he knew his fears were as ridiculous as his dream had been, he tied his robe at the waist and sauntered over to the table, saying, "So, you decided to fix your own breakfast, eh? I didn't realize you girls were so grown up. Sorry I slept so late, but you could have woke me up. Guess it's too late to go to church. Gran'll give us a lecture."

Lizzie and Maggie stared at him for a minute, unsmiling, then resumed eating their cereal. He stooped to kiss Camilla on the head, then went to the fridge to forage for orange juice. The girls needed a fruit with their breakfast and since they were out of bananas... Trouble was, it seemed they were out of orange juice, too.

"I could have sworn we had another carton of juice," he mumbled to himself.

"We drank the last carton of juice yesterday when Gran made pancakes."

Spencer froze. Was he hallucinating, or had Lizzie just spoken to him? He was almost afraid to turn around. He was certainly afraid to make a reply.

"Dr. Jones? Did you hear me?"

She'd called him Dr. Jones. Now that was reality! If she'd called him Daddy, he'd have known he was dreaming!

He turned around slowly. Cautiously he met Lizzie's surprisingly straightforward gaze. "Yes, I heard you, Elizabeth. You said we drank the last of the juice yesterday...right?"

He waited for a reply, fully expecting not to hear one. But she surprised and delighted him again by saying, "That's right. But Gran put it on the grocery list. She'll buy some tomorrow. There's powdered drink mix on the counter by the toaster."

Lizzie returned to her cereal and Spencer forced himself not to jump up and down with glee. This was wonderful! This was *progress!* But he didn't dare overreact. He knew instinctively that he'd ruin everything if he got all excited, ran over to Lizzie and danced her around the room, shouting, "You talked to me! You talked to me!"

He turned to face the counter again, found the can of powdered drink, took three small plastic glasses and a training cup out of the cupboard and mixed the drink and cold water with a shaky hand. While no one could see him, he allowed his grin to stretch from ear to ear. Then, schooling his expression into something a little less jubilant, he turned around and carried the drinks to the table, two in each hand.

He placed a drink by each girl, sat down, then picked up the front page section of the newspaper and unfolded it in front of him, inquiring casually, "Anything look good in the funny papers this morning?"

There was no immediate reply and he nervously peered around one edge of the paper at Maggie. She caught his eye, widened her own eyes and gave a little shrug, then shifted her gaze to Lizzie. Peering around the opposite edge of the paper, Spencer observed that Lizzie was busily scooping out the last of her sugared milk at the bottom of her cereal bowl.

He felt his hopes plummeting. Maybe he was rushing her. Maybe he should have waited till she'd said something else. Maybe—

Lizzie suddenly looked up, her cheeks rather pinker than usual and finally answered, "Garfield looks funny. I can read some of the words, but not all of them."

Spencer was instantly elated again. He couldn't help a quick, ecstatic grin in Maggie's direction when Lizzie ducked her head to take a sip of her drink. Maggie grinned back. Apparently she, like Spencer, had felt that the orange juice conversation was promising but not conclusive. Now she appeared to be building up her courage to speak, too. It wasn't that she was afraid to speak to Spencer, she just wasn't sure whether or not her older sister would approve.

Watching Lizzie cautiously, Maggie ventured, "Maybe you could read Garfield to us, Dr. Jones."

Lizzie looked up again, met Maggie's gaze first, then Spencer's. He realized at that moment that despite her matter-of-fact tone of voice, Lizzie was feeling shy and uncomfortable, as attested to by her flushed cheeks. He ached to let her know how much he appreciated this effort she was making, to tell her he understood how difficult it was. But he couldn't. It would be too much, too soon. So, instead, he just smiled at her.

And Lizzie smiled back.

As far as Spencer was concerned, that smile was a miracle that ranked right up there with the parting of the Red Sea. He was one happy man!

"So, what do you think, Elizabeth? You want me to read Garfield to you?"

Her delicate brows knitted thoughtfully. "No."

His smiled wavered.

"I want you to read the *whole* funny papers."

His smile stretched from ear to ear again, and he didn't hide it from anyone.

A half hour later, after he'd read the funny papers to the girls on the library sofa—Lizzie and Maggie cuddled up to him instead of sitting carefully apart— they all went upstairs to change into play clothes for a trip to the park. The older girls could manage dressing without help as long as there weren't a lot of buttons and bows and stuff, so Spencer was free to dress Camilla Rose, place her in her playpen with a few favorite toys, then go to his own room to slip into jeans and a sweatshirt.

It was during those few quiet minutes away from the girls, his whole being still warm with gratitude and happiness, that Spencer allowed himself to think of Alexandra. Oh, it wasn't that he hadn't thought of her before. Her image, her essence had intruded all morning long. He'd have been thinking of her even if the girls hadn't decided to talk to him that morning, but the fact that he owed his present happiness to her made it impossible not to think of Alexandra constantly…and with very conflicted feelings.

He sat on the end of the unmade bed and pulled on a pair of tube socks, picked up one of his tennis shoes, then just stared into space. Obviously Alexandra had been telling the truth when she said that her conversation with the girls had gone just as she'd initially reported. There was no other explanation for Lizzie's sudden willingness to talk. Maybe she'd come to Jonesville with some other ending in mind, but somewhere along the way Alexandra had changed her mind about that ending and made it a happy one for him and the girls.

He frowned and tugged on his shoe. But that didn't excuse all her initial deceit, did it? He realized she probably thought she was acting in the best interest of her nieces, but— He blinked and stopped in the middle of tying his shoe when he realized that he really didn't know what Alexandra thought or what had motivated her behavior. Every time she'd started to confess or explain last night, he'd either kissed her or, later on, cut her off with some sarcastic or hurtful remark.

Those kisses had been incredible….

He shook his head and shoved on the second tennis shoe with more force than necessary. So what if the kisses were incredible? And what did it matter what her motivation had been to act the way she'd acted? Did the end justify the means? He was done with deceitful women, women he couldn't trust. Besides, she'd used him.

Just like you used Bernice, his conscience taunted him.

But that was different, Spencer reasoned.

Was it?

Tired of fruitless conversations with his conscience and ready for some playtime with the girls, he stood up and moved to the door just as the girls burst in after a very short knock.

"Are you ready, Dr. Jones?" Maggie asked him, her cheeks rounded in a huge smile. "I want you to push me really, *really* high in the swing, okay?"

Spencer tapped her nose. "Okay, sweetie." He smiled at Lizzie. "You, too, Elizabeth?"

Lizzie nodded, shy and eager at the same time. "Yes. Then we can do the seesaw and the merry-go-round. But first we have to pick up Gran and Alex."

Spencer should have been prepared for this. He should have known the girls would be asking for Alexandra because she'd told them she wouldn't be going back to Boston till later today. But he wasn't prepared and he didn't have a clue what to say.

"Well, we can pick up Gran if she's home from church, but—"

"No need to pick me up," Gran announced as she appeared at the door behind the girls. "Where are we going?" *And when did the girls start talking to you?* was the unspoken question in her startled expression.

Spencer winked at her and smiled, and Gran smiled back, her eyes tearing up with happiness.

Just at that moment, Camilla started squealing, obviously annoyed at being left out of the proceedings. Gran went to get her, probably thankful for the chance to wipe her eyes and blow her nose with only baby Camilla Rose as a witness. Meanwhile, Spencer managed, by bending and taking an inordinate amount of time to retie one of his shoelaces, to avoid the girls' question and their searching gazes till Gran got back.

"Where's Alex?" Gran asked the minute she returned.

"Uh…you didn't see her last night?" Spencer stalled. He was hoping Alexandra had talked to Gran last night so he wouldn't have to explain what had happened. Now she, as well as the girls, were waiting for an explanation and he couldn't give them both the same one.

"She left. She went home," he blurted. When Gran opened her mouth to say something, he gave her a warning look. She was just going to have to wait for a more detailed explanation. She got the hint and closed her lips, but she looked concerned. Unfortunately the girls wanted more details, too.

"But she said she wasn't going to leave until this afternoon," Lizzie said, looking distressed.

"She didn't even say goodbye," Maggie wailed.

"I'm sure she would have if she could have, girls," Spencer tried to console them. "But she left…suddenly."

Lizzie stared at him for a minute, looking troubled, then asked, "You didn't send her away, did you?"

This question alarmed Spencer. He remembered what Alexandra had told him last night about Richard sending away the girls' nannies and how Lizzie was worried that he'd act just like Richard if she allowed him to be her daddy. Scared to death that she'd revert to the silent treatment again, he stooped to Lizzie's level, caught her shoulders gently in his hands and looked her square in the eye.

"No, Elizabeth. I didn't send Alex away. I promise you."

With relief, he saw the tension and the worry in her expression ease away. "So, she'll be back? *When,* Dr. Jones? When will Alex be back?"

Her question tore Spencer up inside. He managed a weak smile. "I don't know, Elizabeth."

She looked disappointed, but resigned. She'd feel worse, though, if he told her the truth…that she might never see Alexandra again. That would depend on Alexandra's father, he supposed. It would depend on whether or not Richard Ethington dropped the custody suit and they worked out an arrangement so that the girls could visit him in Boston. If Alexandra wasn't on an assignment in some remote corner of the globe, there was a chance she'd be available to see the girls when they visited their grandfather. They'd probably be delighted to find out she was their aunt.

In the meantime, he had nothing more definite or comforting to tell the girls, so he tried to divert their minds with the prospect of slides and swings and merry-go-rounds at the park.

"Time's a' wasting, girls," he exclaimed as he stood up. "Better take your jackets in case it gets nippy before we head home. Thought we'd grab lunch at McDonald's. How's that sound?''

It must have sounded good because the girls hurried away to get their jackets and the problem of explaining an absent Alexandra was put off for a while. By the look on Gran's face, however, Spencer knew his grandmother wasn't going to be put off for long or diverted so easily.

He was right. After a fun-filled hour and a half at the park, they went to the nearest McDonald's, which was over in Lancaster. Camilla Rose fell asleep in Spencer's arms after a bottle and some French fries, but Lizzie and Maggie, revived by hamburgers and chocolate shakes, were taking advantage of the small play area attached to the fast-food restaurant.

As they watched the girls play, Spencer wasn't surprised when Gran brought up the subject of Alexandra. But her first question was a surprise.

"Did she sleep at your house last night?"

"No, she didn't."

Gran sniffed. "Well, she didn't sleep in *my* house. You don't need to pussyfoot around with me, Spence. I've seen the way you two look at each other."

Spencer sighed. "We weren't together, Gran. As far as I know, she didn't even sleep in New Hampshire last night. She went back to Boston."

She peered at him in confused disbelief. "*Last night?* Why?"

In as few words and with as little emotion as he could manage, Spencer told his grandmother what had happened the night before. She listened till he was finished, then sat silently for some time before remarking, "Well, I'll be a monkey's uncle."

Spencer couldn't help a dry chuckle. "You said it, Gran."

She gave him a sage, sympathetic smile. "Bet you weren't laughing last night. Bet you still feel like hell."

"Listen to you," he teased. "Cussing on a Sunday."

Her smile vanished. "Seriously, Spence. You care about that girl, don't you?"

"I did."

"You *do*."

He said nothing.

"So," she prompted him impatiently, "what are you going to do about this mess?"

"There's nothing to do."

"Sure there is."

"But I don't know what Ethington's going to do, and besides that, she lied to me."

"I expect she thought she had a good reason."

"Does that make it right?"

"I suppose not. But people make mistakes, Spence. Big ones, little ones. And I'd say this one's mighty small compared to what Karlie did to you."

"I'm not comparing her to Karlie, if that's what you're implying," Spencer retorted.

"Sure you are. You compare all women to Karlie. You can't help it."

"Well, if that's true, this one's too much like her."

"Why? Because you love her, just like you loved Karlie?"

"Yes. *No.*" Spence rubbed his temple. "Gran, you're confusing me."

"I'll grant you the right to be confused and, yes, hurt right now. But don't wallow in it too long. She'll be off to Afghanistan or Siberia or some other far-off place before you know it. Reachin' out and touchin' someone is harder than the TV commercial makes it sound. Cell phones don't work in Timbuktu. Least, I don't think they do…"

Exasperated, he demanded, "What makes you think she even wants to hear from me?"

"How can you even ask that, Spence? You two are stuck on each other."

"But her father's still a problem. If he pursues custody of Margaret and Camilla Rose, there'll be a fight. Whose side will she be on?"

"Well, I can tell you this much, Spence. Alex and I have talked about her father a bit, and she's crazy about him. I'm sure her love for, and her loyalty to, her father was the main reason she came here in the first place. But, after she'd been here a spell, she knew the girls belonged with you and, despite daughterly devotion, she decided to risk her father's disapproval and help you and the girls become a family. If it weren't for her, you'd still be waiting for the girls to talk to you. I'd say she deserves some credit for that and should have been listened to last night when she tried to explain instead of being sent away."

"Gran, I didn't send her away!"

"Not in so many words, but—" She shrugged and sighed. "I think it's time to go home, don't you?"

Gran got up and went to gather the girls, leaving

Spencer with his uncomfortable thoughts. Had he really sent her away? Was he like Richard in that way? Had he found fault with her, then decided to disregard all the good she'd done, all the goodness she was capable of?

When they got back to the house, Spencer put Camilla in her crib and Gran took the girls back to her house to make Halloween cookies for Lizzie's kindergarten class.

As he was slowly descending the stairs, deep in troubled thought, the doorbell rang. When he answered the door, he found Richard Ethington standing on his porch, looking as grim as a grave digger.

"I know what you're thinking," Ethington growled. "*Him* again. But we've got to talk, Jones."

WHEN ALEX HAD RETURNED to her apartment last night, there had been a message on her answering machine from an editor who wanted pictures for a magazine spread having to do with the recent cease-fire in the Basque country of Spain. It seemed like a reasonably safe time to get in there for pictures of the people and the country that had been embroiled for such a long time in political and religious unrest. She'd called the editor back first thing that morning and taken the job.

After she hung up with the editor, she'd called her dad. Of course, he wasn't happy that she was going away again. He'd questioned her motives for taking a job so far away and for so long—an estimated two months.

"It's my job, Dad," she'd told him with a warning tone in her voice. She knew he thought she was running away. Running away from Spencer and her feelings. But that wasn't the case. Well...even if it was, it was her business and nobody else's.

Her dad had backed off and offered to drive her to the airport Monday morning. She'd agreed and said goodbye, then went into her bedroom to unpack her suitcase from her trip to New Hampshire and repack for her trip to Spain. But when she came across her cameras, she decided to develop pictures instead.

By the time dusk settled over the city, Alex was sitting in her living room with the photos she'd developed spread out on the sofa beside her. She couldn't seem to quit looking at the images of her ill-fated trip to Jonesville. For being so ill-fated, she had many wonderful memories.

There were pictures of Camilla taking her first steps, her face alight with pride and excitement, her eyes beaming as they rested on her daddy...Spencer, with his arms held out to her.

Then there was Spencer dancing Camilla around the room, his smile brimming with fatherly affection.

There was Spencer again, at the Fords', holding their baby in his big, capable hands directly after the birth, awe and relief and gratitude etched on his handsome features.

There were Dolly and Josh, tired and spent, but ecstatic as they held their cleaned-up bundle of joy.

Then there were Elizabeth and Margaret in their Halloween costumes, fairy-tale beauties in spangled net skirts, ribbon sashes and crowns made out of gold-glittered cardboard.

Camilla, waddling around in her duck costume.

Irma, posing with her broom and thrusting her warted nose close to the camera.

Bernice, as Dorothy from the Wizard of Oz, looking at the camera— and the photographer—with suspicious eyes.

And Spencer as Zorro... That one sent chills down Alex's spine. Her memory hadn't been exaggerating how handsome he'd looked in that dashing costume. How sexy...

And, finally, pictures of Spencer bathing Camilla, his lean, muscled forearms flecked with suds, the dark blond hair wet and slick against his brown skin. That picture sent chills down her spine, too.

Alex sighed and dropped the last picture into the pile. *Every* photo of Spencer sent chills down her spine. And all the other photos, the candid shots of townspeople, the town itself, the surrounding beauty of the New Hampshire hills and forests, made her feel a pang of homesickness like she'd never experienced before.

She'd been restless and roaming her entire adult life, traveling to distant countries, digging into their cultures and living with their people. Searching, she realized now. Searching for a place she'd feel comfortable staying for more than a few weeks at a time. Searching for roots. For *home*.

But maybe home wasn't so much a place as a feeling. A feeling of belonging with certain people. Or belonging to a certain *person*.

Unwelcome tears stung Alex's eyelids as she thought about Spencer. How had this happened? She'd miraculously found the man of her dreams, the home and family she'd been unconsciously searching the world for, then she'd blown the whole thing...in just a few days!

If only she could borrow Bernice's ruby slippers, click the heels together and wish herself back "home" in Spencer's house, in Spencer's arms.

But wishing and regretting and feeling sorry for herself did not get the packing done, Alex finally told herself sternly. If she was going to get on with her life, make a fresh start, that would have to include a well-packed suitcase with plenty of clean underwear, warm socks, several pair of jeans—

En route to the bedroom, Alex's doorbell rang. She stopped, considered, then moved to open it. It had to be her dad. Since she was on assignment and away from home so often, the small group of friends she had in Boston knew better than to just drop by without calling first.

She ran a hand through her tousled hair and straightened the stretched neck hole of her oversize T-shirt, which had fallen down over one bare shoulder. Her father would take one look at her and offer to buy her some new clothes, she thought ruefully.

Determined to hide how sad she'd been feeling, she smiled brightly and began the teasing banter even as she was opening the door. "Don't try offering me another million, Dad. Money's nice, but a date with Brad Pitt...now there's something that might persuade me to stay at least one more—"

She stopped abruptly when she realized that, instead of her father, someone even cuter than Brad Pitt was standing outside her door.

Chapter Thirteen

"Spencer...."

He was dressed in a nice pair of gray slacks, a burgundy sweater and loafers. Not too dressed up, but not his usual casual style, either. He managed to looked darned good in whatever he wore, though, whether it was a white lab jacket, a black cape with a matching mask and assorted sinfully sexy accessories, cords and jeans, or crazy ties and loud boxer shorts.

He was still tall, blond and devastating. He still made her heart beat like a Ricky Ricardo bongo solo. He still made her wish she hadn't lied to such a decent guy and make the fatal mistake of falling in love with him.

But the hard, cold expression on his face when she'd left him last night was gone. Today he looked open, even a little apologetic. Did she dare to hope he'd forgiven her and had come to say so? What was he doing there?

"You're probably wondering what I'm doing here," he said with a sheepish smile, as if reading her thoughts.

When she didn't answer, but simply stood there

like a not particularly well-clothed statue, he raised a tawny brow. "Can I come in, Alex? I'd like to talk to you."

She crossed her arms over her chest, felt taut nipples pressed against her T-shirt, then realized and remembered for the first time that she wasn't wearing a bra. This just added to her confusion and embarrassment and she could barely articulate the necessary words to invite him in. But, damn it, she did want him to come in.

"Oh. Er...sure. Come in." She stood aside and waved him through, then suddenly remembered something else...her pile of photographs on the sofa. As he walked into the living room, she hurried after him, her mind frantically searching for a possible explanation to give for why she'd developed the pictures almost the minute she'd arrived home. She was coming up with nothing and was wondering if he'd think it was strange if she launched herself over the back of the sofa and sat down on the photos, hiding them under the long hem of her T-shirt.

But before she could act on this desperate measure, he saw the pictures, recognized his own image prominent among them, then sat down on the sofa and picked up the one on top—the one of him bathing Camilla—without asking a single question or making a single remark. Alex was left with nothing to do but watch, her arms still crossed uneasily over her chest, as he slowly looked through the entire collection, a smile—sometimes tender, sometimes amused, sometimes embarrassed—constantly curving his lips.

The smile he wore when he finally looked up at

her was warm. "You really are a good photographer."

She shrugged, dropped her arms to her side, remembered her lack of supportive underwear and recrossed her arms. "Thank you. But, in this case, I had such wonderful subjects."

His eyes widened slightly, and she hastily added, "The girls, you know. They couldn't possibly take a bad picture."

"I won't disagree with you there."

She nodded, smiled nervously, then quickly sat down in a chair across from the sofa at the opposite end. She grabbed a throw pillow and casually hugged it against her chest.

He watched her with disconcerting closeness. The room felt too warm, too small. Her skin tingled and her nipples, thankfully hidden behind the cushion, continued to stand at attention like a couple of eager recruits.

She spoke first. "What…what did you want to talk about, Spencer?"

"The girls."

Of course, the girls. Why had she half hoped he might be there to talk about him and her? But there was no him and her, she sternly reminded herself. He might not be angry enough to toss her to the wolves anymore, he might even be ready and willing to forgive her for her deception, but she mustn't allow herself to cherish silly hopes about renewing their didn't-get-a-chance romance.

"Then it's my father's living room you should be sitting in," she suggested softly. "And, while I can't speak for him, and I don't know when or how he plans to tell you, I think you'll like what he has to say. And I can pretty much guarantee he won't shout or thump his fist against the furniture." She gave a small, crooked smile. "He doesn't always speak just a decibel below the roar of a rocket launch, you know. In fact, he's not such a bad guy if only you two would sit down and—"

"We did."

"What?" Alex sat forward, causing the cushion to drop to the floor. She quickly retrieved it, probably drawing more attention to her chest than if she'd just brazened out the no-bra situation. His brows puckered slightly in a puzzled expression. Enlightenment, then amusement, dawned in his sky-blue eyes. He tried not to smile.

"You were saying you talked to my father?" she prompted him, her cheeks glowing with warmth.

He nodded, gallantly composed his urge to comment on her predicament, and explained, "Your father flew up to see me today."

Alex's eyes widened. "He didn't waste any time."

"No, and I'm grateful for that. He informed me that he will make his first order of business tomorrow morning dropping the custody suit. We talked and came to an agreement concerning the girls."

She smiled, forgetting her embarrassment in the sheer joy of the moment. "And just what did you and my Mr. Big Shot Millionaire father agree to?"

He smiled back, again a little sheepish. "We agreed that the further involvement of attorneys was unnecessary. We agreed that I will still retain sole custody of the girls and formally adopt them. But we also agreed that the girls will be told—in fact, they've already been told—that your father is their biological grandfather, a part of the family, and he can be as big a part of their lives as he wishes.''

She raised both brows. ''As he wishes?''

Spencer chuckled. ''Your father knows there'll be limits. The same limits any parent would insist on when dealing with a grandparent used to getting his own way and with a tendency for overindulgence.''

''You've noticed that already?'' she observed wryly.

''Yes, I've noticed. It's a wonder you're not spoiled rotten.''

Alex agreed with a smile and a nod, then lapsed into silence. They'd talked about the girls, so now what?

Spencer was silent, too, but he seemed to be gearing up for something big. She figured that something big was an acceptance of the apology she'd offered last night and an expressed hope that, if for no other reason than the girls, they could be ''friends.''

Of course she would agree. But she could only be friends with him from the distance of whatever country she was sent to, not in close quarters like these. A friend didn't feel for another friend what she felt for Spencer Jones. A friend wouldn't want to tackle him and make love to him till he had to administer lifesaving C.P.R. on himself. A friend wouldn't be writing off every other man in the universe as an impossible, subpar substitute. A friend wouldn't want to marry him and have his babies.

But she'd accept his offered friendship, anyway, resolving to do so with dignity and a reserved gratitude.

He sat forward on the sofa, his elbows on his knees, his hands tightly clasped in front of him. He looked at those clasped hands for a couple of minutes, then lifted his gaze to Alex's face. She prayed her emotions weren't written there for all the world and Spencer Jones to read.

"Lizzie and Maggie are talking to me."

She leaped off the chair, forgetting her dignity and her cushion. "Oh, Spencer, I'm so glad," she exclaimed as she threw her arms around his neck and hugged him. "You must be so happy!"

She felt his hands instantly grasp her waist and his wide shoulders rise as he stood up and pulled her close. "I'm even happier now," he confessed, his warm cheek resting against hers and his breath tickling her ear.

She placed her hands against his hard chest and drew back, gazing up at him, wide-eyed. "I'm sorry. I got carried away. I didn't mean to—"

"I'm glad you got carried away," he growled. "I was wondering how I was going to get you into my arms after behaving like such a jackass last night."

"Oh, Spencer, you had every right to feel the way you did. I was wrong and I—"

"You apologized. I should have let you explain—"

"But you were in shock. And so were we, really. To find out that Elizabeth is yours! I'd never have guessed. You always treated them equally."

"I love them. All three of them."

"I know you do. You'll make a perfect daddy. You *are* a perfect daddy."

He made a grimacing smile. "They still call me Dr. Jones, except, of course, for Camilla. But I think they'll come around in time. Especially if you agree to help out."

That's when it hit her that she wasn't going to be near enough to help out. "Spencer, I've agreed to take an assignment in Spain."

"I know. Your father told me. I have a feeling that's why he wasted no time in getting to me with his decision about dropping the custody suit. He was itching to quickly fix things between me and him so he could tell me about your plans to skip the continent tomorrow." He tucked her close against him and smiled into her face. "He flew me down here in his plane. Then he offered me a million bucks if I'd convince you to call back that editor and tell him you'd got a better offer."

She smacked his shoulder. "You're lying!"

He chuckled. "Yes. I'm lying. I accepted his offer of a ride in his private jet, but he knew he wouldn't have to pay me a plug nickel to try to convince you to stick around for a while."

"So I could help you with the girls?"

"That would be a nice bonus, but you know I've learned my lesson about wooing women just for their mothering skills." He lifted his hands and squeezed her shoulders. "Look, Alex, I know that magazine editor won't be able to wait for the best photographer in the world—namely you—and he'll be forced to give the assignment to someone else if you don't take it, so I can understand if you really have your heart set on it. But if you'd hold off on your world travels for just a short while, Alexandra, you and I could get to know each other a little better."

"Alexandra! You called me Alexandra."

"I know."

"My mother always used my full name, but no one else does. You've *never* called me that before."

"I've always wanted to. I've always thought of you as Alexandra. And I've always imagined saying it out loud just before doing this."

His arms slid around her back again. Tightening the embrace, he bent his head and kissed her. Alex could feel the pent-up emotion in his kiss. His lips were gentle, yet demanding. The feel of his tongue inside her mouth sent shivers through her body. Her response was just as passionate, just as full of feeling.

Spencer's long, hard body pressed to hers set her head to spinning, her heart to pounding. Oh, how she loved him! And how she wanted him! Now, more than ever.

He drew back and cupped her face, then smiled into her eyes, his own eyes hazy with longing…and love?

"I don't want to scare you, Alexandra Koskov. And I don't want to make you feel pressured, but—"

"But what?" she breathed.

"I know I've only known you since Friday, since that fateful day when you crossed those gorgeous gams while sitting on my examination table." His teasing tone softened, grew serious. "I love you, Alexandra."

Alex's blood thrummed through her veins like an elixir of joy. *He loved her!* If he only knew how much those three little words, and how little that job in Spain, meant to her right now! Sure, she loved being a photographer. And she'd enjoyed her travels and all the wonderful experiences she'd had, the people she'd met. She didn't regret a minute of it.

But when she'd looked into her heart earlier that day, she'd realized that she'd been looking for something intangible in the tangible realities of her work. And now she'd found that intangible something in Spencer's arms, in the joys of a family. In Jonesville, New Hampshire, of all places! And the last two days had proven that she could find great photo opportunities without traveling to the ends of the earth and missing out on the pleasures of home and family.

"Well, guess what, Spencer Jones. I love you, too," she informed him with a coy grin. "And I think I like the idea of sticking closer to home and getting to know you a little better."

His smile was jubilant. "Man, am I ever having a good day."

So was Alex. And it was just getting better and better. Now Spencer was stroking her neck with his long, beautiful fingers, kissing her eyes, the curve of her jaw, the shallow cleft in her chin. He nibbled his way down her neck, slipping the opening of her T-shirt down till the soft, sensitive skin of one shoulder was exposed. He kissed her bare shoulder while he slipped his hands under her T-shirt, over her hips, along her waist, then found her breasts at last, heavy and aching with need.

A tiny moan escaped Alex's throat as he cupped her, then gently stroked the nipples with the pads of his thumbs.

"You tried to hide these from me when I first got here," he murmured.

"I didn't want you to see how much just the sight of you excited me," she returned on a gasp.

"Well, your cover is blown, sweetheart. I've got more than an inkling of how much I excite you."

She chuckled into his mouth. "Smug man."

"Hey, you didn't let me finish."

"Oh, you're going to finish all right."

He choked on a laugh. "Tease. I was going to tell you that I'm even more excited than you are."

"Wanna bet?"

"Is that a dare?"

"No, Spencer Jones. That's a invitation to get to know me a little better. Isn't that why I'm calling my editor right away to cancel my trip?"

He groaned. *"Right away?"*

"Okay, in an hour, then."

"Two hours."

She bit his ear. "Have you seen my bedroom?"

"No, but I'd liked to."

She wriggled out of his grasp and grabbed his hand, pulling him toward the hallway that led to her bedroom with a smile on her lips and mischief in her eyes. "Good, because that's the best room in the house for playing doctor."

Spencer returned her grin with a sly one of his own and meekly allowed himself to be led away.

TWO AND A HALF MONTHS later, on New Year's Day, most of the population of Jonesville, New Hampshire, a large part of Lancaster and surrounding neighborhoods left their unlocked houses exposed to the possible dangers of large-scale looting as they flocked to the church on the town square for the wedding of Dr. Spencer Jones to Alexandra Koskov Ethington.

There were the inevitable mourners in the group, mostly the nanny wanna-bes and other sundry single females coming from as far away as Dixville Notch—even a few uninvited—to dab their eyes through the ceremony that would put the eligible doctor out of their reach forever.

And there was no doubt in anyone's mind that this was one of those unique "forever" marriages. The bride and groom were, as Gran liked to put it, "ga-ga" for each other.

Fortunately, Bernice Galloway was not one of the mourners. She and Leonard Steinfeldt were engaged and planning a Valentine's Day wedding. Alex and Bernice had become friends and there were no hard feelings on the part of Spencer's former small-town sweetie.

Myra Henderson was in attendance, carrying, as usual, her brightly covered cushion to soften the misery of sitting on a hard pew for half an hour. She smiled through the entire ceremony, frequently telling anyone who would listen—in a very loud whisper—that she was the one responsible for Spencer and Alex getting together. After all, if she hadn't found a seat for Alex in Dr. Jones's waiting room that day a few weeks ago when she came in to get birth control pills, they might never have married!

Dolly and Josh Ford were there with baby Amelia and their army of boys, taking up most of a pew. Josh took credit, too, for forwarding the romance between Spencer and Alex, but said he couldn't divulge particulars, saying only that "sharing shelter during a storm, delivering a baby and sleeping on a cabin floor in front of a fire on top of a mountain was enough to make anyone feel romantic.'' Then he'd wink.

Kathy and Pete Anderson were there with their five teenagers, her belly as round as a basketball and her face wreathed in a huge smile. She said she couldn't take credit for Spencer finding romance, but Spencer could certainly take credit for her happy pregnancy. Then, when she got strange looks, she'd blush and explain. ''He's not responsible for the *pregnancy,* you understand, just for me being *happy* about it!''

Pete just laughed his head off and kissed his glowing wife on the cheek.

Velma was there, too, making sure the wedding and reception went off according to plan. She had been a godsend to Alex, helping with all the details that went with planning a wedding, from the invitations to the decorations to the cake to the champagne. She was happy to help, glad to see Spencer settling down. She approved of his choice of a bride and could now throw out all those nanny applications and would, hopefully, be getting fewer calls from infatuated females.

As for the bride, Alex felt like a princess in an elegant Donna Karan gown she'd fallen in love with at a bridal boutique in Boston, but had at first declined to buy after seeing its hefty price tag. Her father, however, insisted that she have exactly what she wanted, because, after all, she was only going to be married once, she was his only daughter and since she wouldn't let him throw her the biggest wedding extravaganza in the history of Boston society, she must at least allow him to buy her the gown of her choice!

Alex was no proof against these arguments...and was secretly glad she'd caved in. Next to a tuxedoed Spencer, always so dashing in black, she had to hold her own!

Elizabeth and Margaret were flower girls, little enchantresses in white taffeta with wreaths of daisies in their hair. Camilla was too little to walk down the aisle on her own—she was too easily distracted—but her grandfather, big and square-shouldered and proud as a peacock in his own fine designer feathers, carried her in his arms as she tossed flowers into the congregation, only occasionally hitting someone in the eye.

Gran was Alex's maid of honor and Spencer's handsome father stood up for his son. The wedding party was small, but the congregation was vast, squeezed into the moderate-size church up to the rafters.

As she exchanged vows with Spencer, Alex thought she'd never known such happiness. But even that solemn and joyous moment was outshone, in her opinion, by a conversation she and Spencer overheard during the reception that was held afterward in both their house and Gran's, with awnings stretched between the two buildings so guests could switch locations comfortably.

This conversation occurred in the library while Alex and Spencer, who was holding Camilla, chatted with one of his two older sisters. Elizabeth and Margaret stood nearby, sipping punch, carefully holding their cups like little ladies in an effort to keep their lace gloves and white frocks as pristine as when they'd put them on.

A patient of Spencer's, a well-dressed, elderly gentleman, spotted the girls and was evidently charmed. He bent down to pat Elizabeth on the cheek, saying, "My, aren't you and your sister quite the little ladies. What's your name, my dear?"

Prettily polite, Elizabeth answered, "My name is Elizabeth." She turned and smiled up at Spencer. "But my daddy calls me Lizzie. Don't you, Daddy?"

Margaret, not to be outdone, beamed and poked her chest. "And Daddy calls me Maggie."

Spencer chuckled and stooped to gather them close. With Elizabeth and Margaret in the circle of his arms, Camilla Rose perched on his knee, and Alex standing by his shoulder, he announced happily, "What I call all four of you wonderful females is the biggest and best surprise of my life."

HARLEQUIN®

A M E R I C A N ◆ R O M A N C E®

A special feeling,
  A special secret...
    No one blossoms more beautifully
      than a woman who's

With Child...

And the right man for her
will cherish the gift of love she brings.

Join American Romance and four
wonderful authors for the event of a lifetime!

THAT'S *OUR* BABY!
Pamela Browning
March 2000

HAVING THE BILLIONAIRE'S BABY
Ann Haven
April 2000

THAT NIGHT WE MADE BABY
Mary Anne Wilson
May 2000

MY LITTLE ONE
Linda Randall Wisdom
June 2000

Available at your favorite retail outlet.

HARLEQUIN®
Makes any time special ™

Visit us at www.romance.net

HARWC

Your Romantic Books—find them at

www.eHarlequin.com

Visit the *Author's Alcove*

➤ Find the most complete information anywhere on your favorite author.

➤ Try your hand in the Writing Round Robin— contribute a chapter to an online book in the making.

Enter the *Reading Room*

➤ Experience an interactive novel—help determine the fate of a story being created now by one of your favorite authors.

➤ Join one of our reading groups and discuss your favorite book.

Drop into *Shop eHarlequin*

➤ Find the latest releases—read an excerpt or write a review for this month's Harlequin top sellers.

➤ Try out our amazing search feature—tell us your favorite theme, setting or time period and we'll find a book that's perfect for you.

All this and more available at

www.eHarlequin.com
on Women.com Networks

HEART OF THE WEST

Every Man Has His Price!

Lost Springs Ranch was
famous for turning young
mavericks into good men.
So word that the ranch was
in financial trouble sent
a herd of loyal bachelors
stampeding back to
Wyoming to put themselves
on the auction block!

July 1999	*Husband for Hire* Susan Wiggs	January 2000	*The Rancher and the Rich Girl* Heather MacAllister
August	*Courting Callie* Lynn Erickson	February	*Shane's Last Stand* Ruth Jean Dale
September	*Bachelor Father* Vicki Lewis Thompson	March	*A Baby by Chance* Cathy Gillen Thacker
October	*His Bodyguard* Muriel Jensen	April	*The Perfect Solution* Day Leclaire
November	*It Takes a Cowboy* Gina Wilkins	May	*Rent-a-Dad* Judy Christenberry
December	*Hitched by Christmas* Jule McBride	June	*Best Man in Wyoming* Margot Dalton

HARLEQUIN®
Makes any time special ™

Visit us at www.romance.net

PHHOWGEN

HARLEQUIN®
AMERICAN ◆ ROMANCE®

presents

CAUGHT WITH A COWBOY

A new duo by
Charlotte Maclay

Two sisters looking for love
in all the wrong places...
Their search ultimately leads them
to the wrong bed, where they
each unexpectedly find
the cowboy of their dreams!

THE RIGHT COWBOY'S BED (#821)
ON SALE APRIL 2000

IN A COWBOY'S EMBRACE (#825)
ON SALE MAY 2000

Available at your favorite retail outlet.

HARLEQUIN®
Makes any time special ™